"You lied to me."

"Some of it was true," Bram disputed.

"You told me *I* proposed to you," Augusta said, "and that isn't true. I remember clearly that *you* proposed, and I turned you down because I was afraid we'd be incompatible."

"Yes, the schoolteacher and the spy. It seemed like it shouldn't make sense. But love isn't a logical thing. Remember the night before I left? We had just made love and you were crying because I had to leave. Remember what you said to me?"

She tried to put the scene together. "I don't think I could live without you now," she said aloud, hearing their voice in her head and repeating the words.

"That's right. And what did you say after that? It was very direct."

Augusta groaned. "I asked you to marry me."

"Yes, you did," he said with obvious satisfaction. "I didn't lie about that."

"But you did lie when you told me we were married three days after we had our blood tests."

"I dreamed," he corrected....

Dear Reader,

Welcome to Harlequin American Romance...where each month we offer four wonderful new books bursting with love!

Linda Randall Wisdom kicks off the month with *Bride of Dreams*, the latest installment in the RETURN TO TYLER series, in which a handsome Native American lawman is undeniably drawn to the pretty and mysterious new waitress in town. Watch for the Tyler series to continue next month in Harlequin Historicals. Next, a lovely schoolteacher is in for a big surprise when she wakes up in a hospital with no memory of her past—or how she'd gotten pregnant. Meet the last of the three identical sisters in Muriel Jensen's WHO'S THE DADDY? series in *Father Found*.

Bestselling author Judy Christenberry's *Rent a Millionaire Groom* launches Harlequin American Romance's new series, 2001 WAYS TO WED, about three best friends searching for Mr. Right who turn to a book guaranteed to help them make it to the altar. IDENTITY SWAP, Charlotte Douglas's new cross-line series, debuts with *Montana Mail-Order Wife*. In this exciting story, two women involved in a train accident switch identities and find much more than they bargained for. Follow the series next month in Harlequin Intrigue.

Enjoy this month's offerings, and make sure to return each and every month to Harlequin American Romance!

Wishing you happy reading,

Melissa Jeglinski
Associate Senior Editor
Harlequin American Romance

MURIEL JENSEN
Father Found

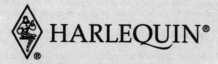

HARLEQUIN®

TORONTO • NEW YORK • LONDON
AMSTERDAM • PARIS • SYDNEY • HAMBURG
STOCKHOLM • ATHENS • TOKYO • MILAN • MADRID
PRAGUE • WARSAW • BUDAPEST • AUCKLAND

To Patricia Teal, agent and good friend

ISBN 0-373-16866-7

FATHER FOUND

Copyright © 2001 by Muriel Jensen.

This edition published by arrangement with Harlequin Books S.A.

® and TM are trademarks of the publisher. Trademarks indicated with
® are registered in the United States Patent and Trademark Office, the
Canadian Trade Marks Office and in other countries.

Visit us at www.eHarlequin.com

Printed in U.S.A.

ABOUT THE AUTHOR

Muriel Jensen and her husband, Ron, live in Astoria, Oregon, in an old Four-Square Victorian at the mouth of the Columbia River. They share their home with a golden retriever/golden Labrador mix named Amber, and five cats who moved in with them without an invitation. (Muriel insists that a plate of Friskies and a bowl of water are *not* an invitation!)

They also have three children and their families in their lives—a veritable crowd of the most interesting people and children. In addition, they have irreplaceable friends, wonderful neighbors and "a life they know they don't deserve but love desperately anyway."

Books by Muriel Jensen

HARLEQUIN AMERICAN ROMANCE

73—WINTER'S BOUNTY
119—LOVERS NEVER LOSE
176—THE MALLORY TOUCH
200—FANTASIES AND MEMORIES
219—LOVE AND LAVENDER
244—THE DUCK SHACK AGREEMENT
267—STRINGS
283—SIDE BY SIDE
321—A CAROL CHRISTMAS
339—EVERYTHING
392—THE MIRACLE
414—RACING WITH THE MOON
425—VALENTINE HEARTS AND FLOWERS
464—MIDDLE OF THE RAINBOW
478—ONE AND ONE MAKES THREE
507—THE UNEXPECTED GROOM
522—NIGHT PRINCE
534—MAKE-BELIEVE MOM
549—THE WEDDING GAMBLE
569—THE COURTSHIP OF DUSTY'S DADDY

603—MOMMY ON BOARD*
606—MAKE WAY FOR MOMMY*
610—MERRY CHRISTMAS, MOMMY!*
654—THE COMEBACK MOM
669—THE PRINCE, THE LADY & THE TOWER
688—KIDS & CO.*
705—CHRISTMAS IN THE COUNTRY
737—DADDY BY DEFAULT**
742—DADDY BY DESIGN**
746—DADDY BY DESTINY**
756—GIFT-WRAPPED DAD
770—THE HUNK & THE VIRGIN
798—COUNTDOWN TO BABY
813—FOUR REASONS FOR FATHERHOOD
850—FATHER FEVER**
858—FATHER FORMULA**
866—FATHER FOUND**

*Mommy and Me
**Who's the Daddy?

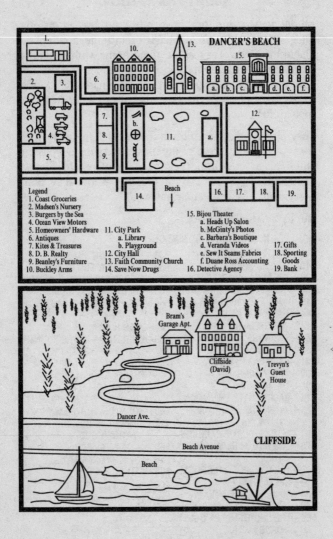

DANCER'S BEACH

Legend
1. Coast Groceries
2. Madsen's Nursery
3. Burgers by the Sea
4. Ocean View Motors
5. Homeowners' Hardware
6. Antiques
7. Kites & Treasures
8. D. B. Realty
9. Beanley's Furniture
10. Buckley Arms
11. City Park
    a. Library
    b. Playground
12. City Hall
13. Faith Community Church
14. Save Now Drugs
15. Bijou Theater
    a. Heads Up Salon
    b. McGinty's Photos
    c. Barbara's Boutique
    d. Veranda Videos
    e. Sew It Seams Fabrics
    f. Duane Ross Accounting
16. Detective Agency
17. Gifts
18. Sporting Goods
19. Bank

Beach

Bram's Garage Apt.

Cliffside (David)

Trevyn's Guest House

Dancer Ave.

Beach Avenue

Beach

CLIFFSIDE

Chapter One

She was going to go insane.

Augusta Bishop stood on the cabin's porch and looked out at the broad green meadow and the evergreen forest beyond, peppered with the crimson and gold of oak and quaking aspen leaves in autumn dress. If she didn't remember who she was in one minute, she thought, she could not be held responsible for what happened. After more than three weeks of this confusion, she had enough pent-up frustration to cut down the forest with her teeth.

"It's like being in the womb," she told herself aloud, rubbing her swollen belly. "An uncertain future stretching out there somewhere, but inside, no past to light the way, just the darkness and the indistinguishable sounds outside."

Dr. Lane had diagnosed the problem as amnesia. She might remember everything tomorrow, he'd said, or she might never recall more than she did at the moment. She retained all her personal skills and her life knowledge, she just didn't remember who she was, where she lived or whom she loved. She thought of it as a Life Saver existence: it could sustain her, but there was a giant hole in the middle.

She walked down the porch steps and part of the way across the meadow, remembering her husband's caution that she not go into the woods.

Her amnesia was the result of an attempt on her life by someone he'd sent to prison, he'd told her, and he'd brought her here to hide in a friend's summer cabin in the mountains of central Oregon.

She looked around her at the magnificent mountains enclosing them in a cozy little valley and was astonished that her mind could ever forget this beautiful image, no matter what kind of injury she'd sustained.

But when Bram had brought her here just over two weeks ago, she'd been certain she was seeing it for the first time.

"We honeymooned here," he'd told her in the rich, quiet voice that seemed to soothe her fears. Unfortunately, it also raised new ones, because she didn't remember him, either.

She'd struggled for weeks to go back as far as her mind would take her, but it refused to go any further than that night three weeks ago when she'd surfaced in the Columbia River, spitting water and wondering what on earth had happened to her. She'd been cold and terrified.

Then the running lights of a boat had appeared and strong male hands had pulled her out of the water.

"What happened?" the man demanded, wrapping

her in a jacket. "I saw your car go in! Were you alone?"

It was as though the questions had struck her ear and then bounced off. She wanted to answer, but she couldn't.

Even as he questioned her, he was on the radio, calling the police. "Astoria police, this is Captain Burgess, pilot boat *Rainbow*. I just fished a young woman out of the water. Saw her car go in right by the church on the Washington side of the river. Have an ambulance meet me at the Red Lion Marina."

He turned the boat around and headed not for the near shore, but for the opposite one, where she saw a mound of lights on the other side of a big bridge.

"What's your name?" he asked her, apparently providing information to the police.

But that was another question that bounced.

She remembered the sense of panic, the jolt to her feet off the cushion in the cabin where he'd placed her. Then the surprise she'd experienced at her sudden awareness of the weight she carried. She was pregnant! More panic blossomed out of itself.

Her name! How could she not know her name?

"Whoa!" The captain had put the radio down and caught her arm, urging her to relax. "It's all right. You're just in shock. Sit down and put that jacket back on. They'll warm you up at the hospital and everything will come back to you."

That had been three weeks ago, and so far, nothing earlier than that moment of surfacing from under water had come back to her.

She sat down awkwardly in the middle of the fragrant grass and listened to the silence. The insects were gone now that it was the second week in October, and all she heard was the rustle of leaves and the steady, staccato sound of Bram's ax against the firewood. Half a mile out of Paintbrush, a town of four hundred, their four-room cabin was on the city water line, but power was iffy depending upon the elements. The only source of heat was a fieldstone fireplace.

The nights were cool now, and Bram said that soon it would snow. He'd been chopping wood for half an hour.

If she was surprised that she'd forgotten the scenery surrounding this mountain meadow, she was astounded that she'd forgotten her husband. When she'd awakened in the hospital the morning after the accident, the hour so early her room was still in shadows, he was leaning over her bed, a finger to his lips asking her to be quiet.

"I'm taking you home," he'd whispered.

Now that she looked back on it, she thought it strange that she hadn't been afraid. She'd looked into his dark brown eyes and seen something there that had reassured her, despite the threatening situation. And the word "home," when she couldn't remember where she belonged, had sounded so inviting.

He'd taken her left hand and held it up to her face, pointing to the simple gold band on her third finger. It had shone in the shadows. He'd placed his hand beside it, to show her that he wore a matching ring.

"I know you don't remember anything," he'd said. "But I'm your husband. You're in danger here, and I want to take you to safety."

The sight of their rings, when she felt so alone, had been a ray of light in her black panic.

Then he'd wrapped her in a blanket, leaped nimbly out the open window and reached in for her.

He was a private detective, he'd told her as they'd driven into the night, and she was a teacher. He'd been working on a case on the Oregon Coast and she'd flown out from their home in northern California to meet him to celebrate his birthday. When it was time for her to return home, they'd left in separate cars, she to drive to Portland and fly home, he to return to work.

He'd been following a small distance behind her on the narrow, winding road along the river, a row of rocks the only protection against the water. He'd seen a car speed out of a side road, then bump the back of her vehicle at high speed. At a low point in the rock wall, the car hit hers again and she went into the river.

Her rescue and resultant amnesia were all over the news.

Bram recognized the car as belonging to the brother of Nicanor Mendez, a trafficker in drugs and women, sent to jail by Bram's testimony.

Bram had been hired by Mendez's wife, who'd suspected infidelity. His surveillance had taken him to Mexico, and when he realized what Mendez was doing, he'd called the DEA.

Certain the man's motive was revenge, and that

he'd see the news and be after her again, Bram had spirited her out of the hospital and they'd been in hiding ever since.

The whole scenario had an unreal quality because she could remember none of it. All the personal things she'd had with her at the time had been lost at the bottom of the river with the rental car.

He'd taken her to their home in Pansy Junction, California, hoping familiar surroundings would help her remember. But they hadn't.

They'd lingered several days for Gusty to rest, but when there'd been two telephone calls with no response on the other end of the line, they'd left stealthily during the night. They'd flown back to Portland, then driven east.

They'd been here ever since in a curious state of suspension. At least, that's how it seemed to her. He'd suggested they occupy separate bedrooms, since she couldn't remember having been intimate with him, and they lived as friends in a state of uncertainty.

As she watched him appear with an armload of wood from around the side of the house, she wondered if their marriage had been in trouble before the accident. They were such different people—or so it seemed to her. He was organized and confident with a tendency to order rather than ask.

And she…well, that was hard to say. She knew so little about herself and her abilities. She'd held her own with him, though she tried to accede to his wishes because of the danger and their unique situation. But she suspected she might be someone who'd never been self-confident. It didn't feel as though that was part of her makeup. She worried about that sometimes, with a baby just five weeks from birth.

What if her memory returned one day and she discovered her marriage had been in trouble? What if she recalled that she'd been about to leave him, or he'd intended to leave her? Then she'd be alone with a baby to support. Then what?

Bram said she'd been a teacher, but with no knowledge of her past, how could she return to her old job, or sell herself and her skills to a new school board? No. She'd have to think of something else.

She could cook. She'd learned that over the past few weeks. It didn't seem to matter how little the cupboards held, she apparently had a gift for making something delicious out of nothing.

She was also good in the garden. Bram's friends had planted all kinds of greens, tomatoes, peppers and a veritable field of pumpkins. Then a sudden change of plans had required that they return to the city before Bram and Gusty arrived. Gusty had harvested everything but the pumpkins, which continued to grow.

She'd stashed the vegetables in an old-fashioned root cellar, put up the tomatoes, made green tomato relish with those that hadn't ripened and pepper slaw with the green and red peppers.

She wondered with a hint of black humor whether she'd been a survivalist at some point in her life. Or been stuck alone somewhere in the wilderness.

"A dandelion for your thoughts." Bram squatted

down beside her in the grass and handed her the woolly weed.

She looked into his face and thought, not for the first time, that he was something special. He was tall and muscular, with a presence of strength that had as much to do with internal toughness as with well-defined pectorals and softball-sized biceps.

He had the rugged good looks of a Bogart or a Bronson, his handsomeness defined by harsh features tempered by that reassuring strength. And a bright smile that came seldom and was always a surprise.

Except for the tendency to be a little overprotective and to consider himself in command of their tiny family, he'd been all kindness and consideration since the moment he'd appeared in her hospital room.

He held the dandelion to her lips. "Make a wish," he said with a smile, "then blow on it and tell me what you wished for."

She complied and the cottony wisps flew all around them. Several caught in his side-parted dark hair and she reached up to brush them away. It was strange, she thought, that though she didn't remember their life together at all, she often felt the need to touch him. She wondered if the baby in her womb remembered him and that somehow translated itself to her as her own need.

"I don't think I'm supposed to tell you that," she admonished gently. "Or the wish won't come true."

His dark eyes roved her face, clearly looking for something. "You remember that?"

She tossed the dandelion stem onto the grass.

"That's probably one of those things the doctor said I'd remember, like brushing my teeth, or knowing language." Then something else came to her, unbidden. "Did you know that the word *dandelion* is from an old French phrase meaning lion's teeth. *Dent de lion?*"

He looked surprised. "No, I didn't."

"Yes. Because the spiky leaves on the underside of the floret are like the teeth of a lion." She felt momentarily encouraged by that knowledge, then realized it wasn't technically a memory. She smiled ruefully. "I wonder what my third-graders thought of that information. I must have bored them to death."

"I doubt that very much," he disputed, getting to his feet. Then he reached under her arms from behind her to help her up. "Come on. It's getting too cool for you to sit on the ground. Ready?"

"Bram, I'm fine," she insisted, trying to push his hands away. "There won't be many more days like this, and I'd like to take advantage of it. Did you know that the leaves, roots and flowers are edible, and that they contain calcium and vitamins?"

He ignored her question *and* her protest and lifted her so that she had no choice but to brace her feet under her as he brought her upright.

"I can't believe I married you," she said with a groan of exasperation, "if you pushed me around like this when we were engaged."

"We were never engaged." He put an arm around her shoulders and led her toward the cabin. "We went straight from fighting over everything, to being married. And it was your idea, by the way.''

She stopped in her tracks. ''Never engaged?'' She looked at her ring finger with its simple gold band, then added, ''I don't mean with a diamond, but there must have been a period after you proposed.''

The breeze ruffled his hair as he shook his head. ''Well, if you count the three days we waited for our blood tests and marriage license. And—once again—you proposed to me.''

Bram thought the surprise on her face was almost comical. Not flattering to him, of course, but this time in their lives was not about his ego but her survival. So he'd been demanding and cautious and she didn't always like it, but that was the way it was.

''You're just trying to make me believe that,'' she said suspiciously as they walked back toward the cabin. ''I would never have proposed to you.''

He took her arm where the ground was uneven. ''Why not? You were wild about me.''

She slanted him a suspicious glance. ''I was?''

''You were. Followed me all the way to Portland where I was doing surveillance on a divorce case.''

She stopped again, stubbornly folding her arms over her mounded stomach. He stopped with her, his expression one of indulgent impatience.

''One of the first things I asked you when we went to our house in California was how long we'd been married.''

''Right. And I told you eight months.''

"You also told me we didn't get married because I was pregnant."

"Right again." He grinned. "You got pregnant because we got married. Must have happened on our wedding night. I'm good."

She was trying hard to hold back a smile. "So, I chased you down and proposed to you just because."

"Yes."

"I can't believe I'm like that. I mean, I don't *feel* like the kind of woman who'd follow a man five hundred miles and risk rejection by proposing. I don't think I'm that brave."

He propelled her gently toward the cabin. "That's because you don't remember what it's like to be in love. It gives you power you can't imagine if you've never experienced it—or can't recall it."

"Why did you say yes?" she asked.

He squeezed her shoulders. "Because I was in love, too. And you make the best cookies I've ever tasted."

"Then why didn't *you* propose to *me?*"

"I had, but you'd turned me down."

They were climbing the porch steps, and through a hanging basket of ivy the sun dappled her face. It was a beautiful peaches-and-cream oval, plumped a little by her pregnancy. In it were wide, deep blue eyes, a small, nicely shaped nose, and an expressive mouth that was now parted in interest. Her hair was deep red, and there was lots of it mounded loosely atop her head. The sunlight made it look molten.

"Why?" she asked.

"Because I've been a cop, a soldier, a CIA agent and now a detective, and you said I must have suicidal tendencies to be that reckless. That you wanted a home and children and a husband with a nine-to-five job."

She thought that all over, frowned as though trying to remember it and finally shook her head. "Well, what changed my mind?"

He pushed the cabin door open and ushered her inside. "I like to think it was my winning personality."

She teased him with a smile. "No, really," she said.

He laughed as he picked up the wood he'd dropped onto the porch table and carried it inside. "If that's not the reason, I guess I don't really know. You didn't say. You just asked me to marry you."

She held the door open for him. "Then we were happy?"

She followed him inside and perched on the arm of the pink-and-green-flowered sofa as he lowered the wood into a copper box. That question concerned him. He wanted the circumstance surrounding the birth of their baby to be perfect. He didn't want her to worry about anything.

She hadn't asked that many questions since they'd been here, had mostly occupied herself with preserving the garden's bounty. In fact, she'd dedicated herself to it as though relieved to have something she obviously understood to occupy her mind.

"Yes, we were," he assured her, turning to face

her. "Why? Don't you feel happy? Despite the amnesia, of course."

She looked him in the eye for a long moment and he held her gaze, determined she would read nothing to the contrary there.

She finally shrugged a shoulder and said, almost with apology, "I don't know what it is. Something makes me feel that this…" She waved a hand between him and herself. "That it isn't right. That one of us is—" She gave up trying to explain and shook her head. "I'm not sure what I'm trying to say."

He made an airy stack of three logs, stuffed kindling and rolled-up newspaper in the pocket underneath, then lit it and gave her a quick smile as he reached for the poker.

"You've always had good instincts," he said, giving the top log a slight nudge to open up the air space. "Things aren't right between us. We're usually very affectionate and physical and we have a lot of fun together. This having to sleep apart and treat each other like strangers probably seems wrong to you on some level other than memory. We understand why it has to be, but something elemental in you recognizes it as wrong behavior."

He couldn't tell if she was encouraged or discouraged by his reply.

She got to her feet and came closer to the fire, spreading her hands out as it began to catch. "And I'm affectionate and physical with you even though you're always telling me what to do, or getting in the way of what I want to do?"

He replaced the poker. "You appreciate it as my concern for you."

"That's the honest truth?"

He avoided her eyes as he put the wrought-iron gate back in place. "Yes, it is."

"I'm very tolerant."

"Yes, you are."

She walked into the kitchen on the other side of the fireplace and shouted back at him, "Coffee?"

"Please," he replied as a breath that had been caught in his lungs escaped in a soundless sigh.

"What kind of cookies do I make you?" she called as puttering sounds came from the stove.

"Chocolate chip with pecans are my favorite," he shouted back, turning his back on the small twinge of guilt. "Peanut butter, date bars, this candy thing you call a 'buckeye' that's a peanut butter ball half-dipped in chocolate."

Her head appeared around the doorway. "How come you're not fat?"

He went to lean in the doorway to answer. He pointed to her stomach. "Because you also help me burn the calories."

Her cheeks pinked and she looked just a little flustered. "Insidious of you," she said. "So I get fat instead of you."

"You're always eager to cooperate."

"Says you."

"There again," he said, putting a hand gently to the curve of her stomach, "you bear the evidence."

He should not have touched her. It shocked both

of them—not the shock of surprise, but the electrical charge of a powerful connection.

She'd had a lot to deal with during the past few weeks, and though she'd been very concerned about her memory when he'd taken her to California, the garden had helped relax her when they'd arrived.

But he'd known something had been changing inside her the past few days. She'd been thinking about her place in life as an individual, and about the two of them as a couple. She was worrying about their relationship.

And that worried him.

Her fingers fluttered in the air between them, as though she wanted to touch him but didn't dare. He caught them in his hand and kissed her knuckles, needing to break this spell.

"I'll get the coffee," he said, and walked around her to the coffeemaker.

Though he knew things could not go on forever as they had since he'd taken her from the hospital, he couldn't help wishing they would. She knew only what he wanted her to know.

But the harder she thought, the more likely she was to remember.

Then she'd know what had really happened.

And that would not be good.

Chapter Two

All right, maybe they did have a good thing going.

Gusty examined that likelihood as she added chocolate chips and pecans to the smooth cookie batter. She and Bram had gone into town for plumbing supplies, and she'd picked up a few additional groceries before they headed home. She had game hens and a casserole dish of dressing baking in the oven, potatoes boiling on top of the stove, cauliflower steaming and ice cream in the freezer.

She wasn't sure why she was making the cookies. She couldn't recall having made them for him in the past, but she did have very recent memories of his consideration and his determination to keep her safe, of his taking her to old Dr. Grayson the first day they arrived in Paintbrush, and establishing her last-trimester care. At this point in time there was little she could do to pay him back but provide him with a favorite treat.

Her hands slowed in their work as she remembered the sexual sizzle that had taken place earlier when

Bram had touched her abdomen. She'd felt something ignite inside her and had seen a small explosion in his eyes.

He'd walked around her into the kitchen easily enough, but he had to have felt as affected as she—and she didn't even remember anything they'd shared.

He'd suggested they'd been eager lovers. With what she'd come to know of him—his kindness, despite his insistence on her compliance in matters of her safety—she found that notion both exciting and daunting. She must have had to fight constantly to protect her individuality. And yet she'd married him, so she must have accepted that and found a way to deal with it.

She shifted a little uncomfortably and put a hand to the small of her back as a twinge there reminded her that she'd stood too long.

Sounds of metal clanking on metal came from the bathroom as Bram worked on the plumbing. The iffy nature of the shower had been the cabin's only inconvenience. The water trickled weakly rather than sprayed, and she'd grumbled about it that morning, telling him she longed for a good solid spray against her aching back.

She was touched that he seemed anxious to grant her the wish.

She put more chocolate chips in the batter and, with one hand rubbing her back, folded them in with the other.

Gusty was placing the first pan in the oven when

a male voice behind her said in pleased wonderment, "I thought I smelled cookies!"

She turned to find Bram behind her, a wrench in one grubby hand and a rag in the other.

"I'd give you a bite," she said apologetically, "but they're too hot."

"How about a bite of batter?" he asked hopefully.

She shook her head. "Raw eggs can carry salmonella." She took a few chocolate chips in the tips of her fingers. "Will this do?"

He shrugged. "Better than nothing." He held his dirty hands away from her as she popped the chips into his mouth.

"How's the shower coming?" she asked, offering him a sip of her coffee.

"Mmm. Thanks. I'm just about finished. It was mostly lime buildup. I soaked the head in cleaner and I'm about to reconnect it. If it works, you can have a shower after dinner."

"That sounds wonderful. And the cookies will be cooled by the time you're finished. If it won't spoil your dinner."

"Cookies never spoil anything," he said over his shoulder as he returned to his task.

He had second helpings of everything at dinner, and while she enjoyed her meal also, she knew she'd probably pay for the pleasure with heartburn during the night.

"It seems you married me for my cooking," she observed, sipping at a glass of milk while he carried their plates to the sink.

"That," he said, "and because you were on my mind constantly."

She wondered about that. "Is that the same as love?"

He scraped the dishes and put them in the dishwasher. Coming back to the table for bowls of leftover dressing and potatoes, he gave her a quizzical look. "I thought so. I'm usually very focused and on track. Until I met you and you consumed my life."

She had to ask. "Has that been good or bad for you?"

He grinned and headed for the counter with his burden. "Mostly good," he said.

She laughed lightly. "Mostly?"

She reached for the cauliflower and the rolls, intending to help clear, but his hand came down on her shoulder to hold her in her chair.

"I said I'd clean up." He took the vegetable and rolls from her, then started to cover everything and put it in the refrigerator.

"Mostly," he went on as he worked, "because I used to be focused and on track," he repeated wryly, "and since you came along, I've had to adjust to having my attention split between my work and my life."

"And your life didn't come first when you were a CIA agent?"

Everything put away, he took the ice cream from the freezer and brought down two bowls. "No." He answered matter-of-factly, as though he'd accepted it and didn't particularly regret that now. "Everything about you is secondary to the work. But I was young then and it didn't matter. The men I worked with became my family.''

"You told me you'd already quit the CIA when we met."

"Yes."

He scooped ice cream into the bowls, put the carton away, then brought them to the table, going back for the plate of cookies she'd prepared.

"Then you didn't quit on my account and don't resent me for that?"

He raised an eyebrow as he took his chair again. "No. Why?"

"Because," she said for the second time, "something isn't right between us." When he rolled his eyes impatiently, she raised a silencing hand. "I know, I know. You told me it was because I can't remember, that we're usually very physical and this celibacy is unnatural. But I think it's something else."

SHE PROPPED HER ELBOW on the table and studied him with the disturbing concentration of the innocent. He tried to look back at her with the same innocence.

But he had a feeling she wasn't buying it.

"How can you be so sure," he asked, pushing the cookie plate her way, "when you can't even remember us?"

"It's something I feel now," she said, choosing a cookie and taking a dainty bite out of it. She chewed and swallowed. "I feel as though it's me. There's something about me that you're upset with, or displeased with. Did I do something awful?" She studied the cookie in her hand then looked up at him again, her expression reluctant. ''Did I have an affair, or something?''

Even a hesitation before he answered the question would have given him a break, but he couldn't do that to her. ''No, you haven't had an affair. You've been a wonderful wife.''

She looked somewhat relieved, though not entirely convinced that there wasn't a problem between them. ''You're not just saying that because I can't remember anything?''

''No,'' he said firmly. ''I'm saying it because it's true. We have a good, strong marriage. We're in love.''

''Okay,'' she said finally, then finished off her cookie. ''You told me you have one sister.''

He nodded. ''Lisa. She's in Kansas where her husband's a doctor.''

''Is she older than you?''

''Younger by a year and a half. I have three little nieces.''

She spooned ice cream into her mouth. He took advantage of her distraction to eat some of his own before her interrogation began again. She seemed to be marshaling every detail from their conversations over the past three weeks in a new attempt to force the data to help her remember what had gone before. He managed two bites before she continued.

''And your parents are gone?''

''My father died in jail,'' he replied briefly, trying not to sound bitter or flip. But it was difficult. He *was*

bitter about them, and he always sounded flip when
he tried to pretend that it didn't matter. "My mother
was an alcoholic and finally died of liver failure about
ten years ago."

She looked stunned. He hated that. Then her eyes
filled and he was torn between being touched by her
sympathy, when she didn't even remember him, and
annoyed with himself for upsetting her.

He reached across the table to catch her hand. "It's
all right. Lisa and I adjusted to it long ago. She got
married at sixteen, but to a great guy and they managed to make it work. He got a scholarship, she got
a job and they both worked day and night until he
finally graduated from medical school. He joined a
clinic, and then they had their family."

"And you joined the army after she got married?"

"I was a cop first, then joined the army."

She smiled at that, then frowned again, squeezing
his hand. "I'm sorry about your parents. I can't remember mine, but I don't think I went through anything that awful. You said that I told you they've been
gone for some time."

He ran his thumb over her knuckles. "That's right.
You liked your father, but didn't get along well with
your mother. She was sort of a prima donna, I
gather."

She frowned over that and drew her hand back. It
occurred to him for the first time that since she had
no memories of them, knowing they were gone closed
a door she'd never have a chance to reopen.

She drew a deep breath, clearly regretful. "I don't

remember anything about them, and it makes me feel a little like an orphan.''

He felt a desperate need to cheer her up. ''You still have your sisters.''

She straightened in her chair, suddenly smiling. ''Yes. I'm a triplet. That's different, isn't it? In the photos on my bedside table in Pansy Junction, they look like two clones of me, yet I don't remember them. Where are they again?''

''Athena lives in D.C.,'' he replied. ''She's a lawyer. And Alexis, the artist, lives in Rome.''

She turned the names over on her tongue, saying them over and over, closing her eyes as though that could form an image in her mind. When she opened them again, her eyes were troubled, her bottom lip shaky. ''I don't remember them. Neither of them. And they're probably wondering where I am.''

He hated to tell her the truth here, but he knew he had to. ''I'm sure they are,'' he answered. ''You were all over the news when you were pulled out of the water and didn't know who you were or where you'd come from.''

''That's cruel, isn't it?'' she said urgently. ''They don't know that I'm safe.''

He nodded. ''That was the choice we had to make to keep you safe. Any attempt to call either one could result in our being tracked.''

She settled down, apparently accepting that that made sense.

''I like knowing I have somebody.'' The statement

was plaintively made, as though she desperately needed someone—besides him.

It was interesting, he thought clinically, that no one had been able to hurt him since his mother's ugly drunkenness when he'd come home from school, anxious to tell her about a success only to find her passed out on the sofa. No one, that was, until now.

He'd die without question or hesitation for Gusty and their baby, but she couldn't remember their relationship, was certain there was something wrong with it, and that she needed something more than he could give her.

On some intelligent level, he knew it was foolish to be jealous of her sisters. He loved his own sister very much. They'd sustained each other through the worst times in their lives.

Gusty had turned him inside out over the past eight months, but her safety and the safe arrival of their baby into the world was all he dreamed of, was the reason he'd abandoned everything to hide away with her and keep her from harm.

It was selfish and egotistical, he knew, to want to be her everything, but knowing that and changing how he felt were two very different things.

"You ready for that shower?" he asked, pointing to her abandoned bowl of ice cream. "You can even turn the head now to adjust the spray."

She ignored his question and nibbled on another cookie, looking more composed.

"Am I a good teacher?" she asked.

"There's a Teacher of the Year plaque in your office at home. I pointed it out to you, remember?"

She frowned and gave one nod. "I do, sort of. But home was kind of overwhelming. All those things I'd hoped I'd remember when I saw them, and didn't."

"I think you're good at everything you do," he assured her. "You seem to know all about gardens and cooking." He held up his cookie. "And you're thoughtful. Always trying to help someone, or comfort someone."

She frowned over that. "Am I wimpy?"

He laughed. "As the man who's had to argue with you over just about everything, I can say no to that with authority."

She pushed away from the table. "I guess I'll clean up and have that shower."

He went around the table to help her up. "I'll clean up, you go ahead."

SHE SHOULD HAVE ARGUED, but the prospect of a stream of hot water beating on her sore back was too delicious to delay. She went to her bedroom for the flannel nightgown Bram had bought her in town, then doffed her clothes in the bathroom.

She caught a glimpse of herself in the mirror as she stepped into the shower stall and was a little startled by her size. It was one thing to see herself clothed, and quite another to see her naked, pregnant self.

She stepped into the shower stall, closed the door on the mirror, modulated the water temperature carefully to hot but not too hot, then turned the water on full force. She groaned at the instant relief provided when she turned her back to the spray.

She let it beat for long moments, then got serious about washing. With that accomplished she took the shampoo from the shower caddy and set about the major production of washing her hair. She scrubbed at her scalp, then brought her hair over her shoulder and, starting with the bottom few inches, slowly scrubbed her way up.

She rinsed slowly and carefully, combing her fingers through it to make sure she was rid of all the shampoo. After giving her body one more rinse, she turned off the water.

She put both hands to the sides of the shower as sudden dizziness overtook her. It was almost as though the thrumming of the water had kept her upright, and now that it had stopped, her own rhythms seemed at odds with the universe. She felt as though she might fall at any moment.

She waited for the moment to pass. When it didn't, she forgot all reluctance to be seen naked and shouted for Bram at the top of her lungs.

She heard the bathroom door open in an instant, then the shower door was yanked open and he stood there, a dish towel over his shoulder, his face grim with worry.

"What?" he asked urgently, reaching in for her.

She leaned heavily against him, her head still spinning. "Dizzy," she said.

He pushed the bathroom door all the way open,

yanked a bath towel off the rack and wrapped it around her. "Are you in pain?"

"No."

"You didn't fall?"

"No. But I was...afraid I would. That's why I called you." Leaning against him was a little like lying on a firm mattress. There was solid support against her weary body, and a sense of security that made her want to close her eyes and go to sleep.

"It's like a sauna in here," he said, rubbing her back through the towel to dry it. "You might have just gotten a little carried away now that the shower-head works. The heat built up in this little room and made you feel faint."

"The shower," she said slowly, enjoying the massage, "felt sooo good. My back was hurting."

"Let's get you dried off, and I'll call the doctor." Holding her with one arm, he reached for her robe with the other and put it on her shoulders. Perfunctorily he dried her breasts and belly with the wadded towel.

She didn't know whether to admire or be offended by his clinical detachment when she was suddenly very much aware that she was large and grossly unattractive.

She drew a deep breath of the cool air coming in from outside the room and felt suddenly better. "I don't think that's necessary. You were probably right about..." She hesitated, the breath stuck in her throat as he swiped the towel down her thighs.

"About...the heat in here," she finished haltingly

as he tossed the towel aside and drew her robe together.

As he did so, the baby delivered a strong kick to her abdomen that Bram must have felt against the inside of his arm. He reached inside her robe to flatten his hand against the beach ball of her belly.

She drew in a small breath, aware of every fingertip in touch with her skin, of his intensity as he leaned slightly over her in concentration.

As though recognizing the touch, the baby delivered several more staccato kicks right against the palm of his hand.

"Wow," he said simply, quietly.

His excitement surprised her. "Haven't you felt the baby before?" she asked.

He ignored her a moment, apparently distracted as the baby kicked again. He straightened and helped her out into the living room and onto the sofa.

"It never fails to amaze me," he said, putting a pillow under her head and lifting her feet onto the cushions. "I've watched you grow with the pregnancy, but to actually feel life in there boggles my mind. Still dizzy?"

He covered her with a blanket from his bed, then sat on the edge of the sofa and put a hand to her face.

"No," she said with a sigh. "I'm much better. A little drowsy, maybe. I haven't been sleeping very well."

"I noticed." He disappeared for a moment, then returned with two towels. He placed one under her hair on the pillow, and the other he used to begin to dry it. "I can hear the springs in your bed at night, your trips to the bathroom or the kitchen. You're very restless."

She smiled wryly. "It's tough to carry around all this weight *and* not know who you are."

"You're my wife," he said, rubbing at her hair, "and the baby's mother. Try to hold on to that until your memory comes back."

"You told me we don't know if the baby's a boy or girl."

"Right. We didn't want to know."

"What are we hoping for?"

He cast her a smiling glance as he continued to rub. "One or the other. We're not particular."

"Did we want a baby this soon?"

"It was a surprise," he replied, "but we're very happy about it."

"I feel happy about it." She patted her stomach. A little kick patted her in return. "I just feel sorry that I can't remember learning that I was pregnant, that I can't remember telling you, that I can't remember being excited and shopping for things and…"

"You told me," he said with a laugh, "by putting booties in my shoes." When she looked puzzled, he explained. "I came out of the shower one morning, got dressed and sat on the edge of the bed to put on my shoes and found an obstruction in one of them. It was a yellow bootie trimmed with yellow ribbon. I'm a little thick," he said with a self-deprecating roll of his eyes. "It wasn't until I discovered another bootie in my second shoe that I realized what you were telling me."

"What did we do then?" she whispered, desperately wishing she had that memory.

"We held each other and laughed and cried and I picked you up at school that night and took you out to dinner. We bought a baby names book on the way."

"Have we chosen names?" She struggled to sit up, the weariness falling away.

He helped her and propped a few pillows behind her. "Ah, no. I think you jotted down a few names in the book, but we couldn't come up with anything brilliant and you thought inspiration might strike when you got closer to delivery. But, nothing so far. You're sure you're all right?"

She nodded, then yawned. "I should get up and dry my hair."

"Stay there, and I'll brush it dry for you." He stood to leave and she caught his wrist.

She felt his energy surge through her fingers. "It'll take forever," she said, both touched and alarmed that he'd offer to do that for her. How could she not remember a man who was so devoted to her, whose touch made her feel as though she swung from high-voltage wires?

Or was she right about this unsettling suspicion that all wasn't right between them, and this was intended to convince her that everything was fine, either to speed her recovery or for purposes of his own?

Their gazes locked for an instant. She saw only

attentive kindness in his—then the sudden awareness there that she was uncertain about him. She caught a glimpse of his disappointment before he went into her bedroom and returned with a brush.

"I've watched you do this a hundred times," he said. "It's a brush designed to be easy on wet hair. Close your eyes and think about baby names, and I'll brush."

HE WAS SURPRISED when she complied. He knew she didn't entirely believe him, and he didn't know how to reassure her convincingly. Maybe it was the hormonal riot caused by the pregnancy.

He ran the brush from her scalp, through the fiery length of hair that fell past her shoulder blades when she was standing. It shimmered in the firelight like the darkest part of the flame.

"What about Bailey for a girl?" she asked, her voice quiet.

He made a negative sound. "I hate those last-name first-names."

"Something more ordinary? Like Margaret or Alice?"

"I like Margaret." He remembered a caseworker from some point in his childhood whose name had been Margaret. She'd been middle-aged and a little frumpy, and very kind. "You had talked about using your sisters' names. But you were afraid it might cause too much confusion in the family to have two people with the same name—particularly if a girl turned out looking just like the three of you."

"Alexis and Athena," she thought aloud.

"If we combined them, what would that give us?" she speculated while he brushed. "Athexis?" She laughed.

Her amusement made him smile. She'd had so little to be amused about. "Alena?" he asked. "Lexena?"

"Alena," she repeated thoughtfully. "That's not bad, is it?"

"No, I kind of like that. What if we have a boy?"

She sighed. "A boy. Well, we'd have to name him after you, wouldn't we? Bram..." She stopped, then asked, "What's your middle name?"

"Bramston *is* my middle name." He combed his fingers through her hair to test if he was making progress. Her hair was drying but still damp. "First name, John."

"John Bramston Bishop Jr., if it's a boy?"

"No, I think that causes confusion, too. I think he should have a name that's all his own."

"Okay. Is there anyone you admire that you'd like to name him after?"

"I have a couple of friends who are very important to me. David Hartford and Trevyn McGinty."

"Your CIA friends?"

"Yes."

"David Trevyn Bishop," she said. "Trevyn David Bishop. Sounds pretty good either way. Do you like it?"

"Yeah, I think so."

"Then, let's nail that one down if it's a boy. Maybe with the Trevyn first."

"Works for me. And Alena for a girl? What about a middle name?"

"Alena Marie? Alena Elizabeth? Alena Theresa?" She tried several more combinations that failed to inspire her until she said, "Alena Leanne. Alena... Leanne. Leanne."

"I take it you like that one?" he asked, drawing the brush along the underside of her hair. It was drying now and growing lighter, the copper highlights against the dark red magnificent.

"Bram!" she exclaimed, snapping him out of his sensual study. She reached a hand back to him. "Help me sit up!"

He moved around her to support her to a sitting position. "Dizzy again?" he asked anxiously. "Pain?"

"No." She held on to his arm and pulled him down beside her, her eyes focused on something he couldn't see. "Leanne."

"What about Leanne?" She was making him nervous. He rubbed her back gently.

"I think...I know one. In my classroom." She turned to him suddenly, her eyes brightening, a wide smile forming. "I have one in my classroom!"

Oh God. She was remembering. He tried not to panic. "Leanne who?"

She closed her eyes tightly, the smile becoming a frown. "I don't know. I can't get that part. I can just see...ooh!"

"What do you see?"

"Just..." She fluttered her fingers around herself.

"Lots of blond hair. But no face. She always has her hand up. Leanne. Bram! I remembered something!"

She threw her arms around him, laughing and crying simultaneously. "I remembered something!"

"That's wonderful." From somewhere he found the enthusiasm to force into his voice. "It'll all come back in no time."

She drew away from him, a frown replacing the smile. "But that's so little. No face, no last name, just hair and a hand raised in the air."

He rubbed her shoulder gently. "It is just a little, but if you don't try to force it, it'll come when you're ready."

She made a face at him. "I'm ready now."

That was so her. "Your heart is, but your mind apparently isn't. Let it take the time it needs."

She slumped unhappily, absently patting the baby as though certain it must share her disappointment. If he hadn't loved her before, that gesture would have done it for him.

"Am I usually patient?" she asked

"Yes," he replied. "You teach little children. You have boundless patience."

"Am I patient with you?"

"You don't have to be. I'm the perfect husband." He said it with a straight face.

He thought it might bring a smile to her troubled expression, but it brought a deeper seriousness instead. She studied him closely and he could almost hear her trying to remember something...anything.

"Are you patient with me?" she asked finally.

"Yes. I'm the perfect husband." He couldn't deliver that line twice without cracking a smile.

He was relieved when it finally made *her* smile.

"Okay, you are very patient with me, though we're basically very different. And I try—"

"How are we different?" she interrupted.

He had to be grateful for at least one question that was easy to answer. "I had a childhood that forced me to grow up with few illusions," he said. "And then I was a cop, then a soldier and then a spy. I saw the underside and the back of a lot of things that don't even look good from the front. I'm cynical and hardnosed with a real preference for things done my way."

She looked genuinely puzzled. "I haven't gotten that impression at all. Except for the things-done-your-way part." She added the last with a grin.

"I've been on my best behavior." That was true. If she caught a glimpse of the real Bram Bishop, it might trigger the return of her memory sooner rather than later and he'd be dead in the water. "You, however, are gentle and kind, trusting, optimistic, a Pollyanna for the new millennium."

She winced. "It's generous of you to exaggerate my good qualities. I'm sure I have some bad habits."

He shrugged. "You love to argue with me."

That seemed to deepen her amusement. "Maybe that's a good quality, too. Maybe it's a way to defend myself against your need to control. Even if I love you, maybe I don't want to be taken over by you."

"I don't want to take you over," he insisted. "I just want to keep you safe and happy."

"Maybe what you want for me isn't the same thing I want for myself."

She knew that was it. She saw it in his face, though he averted it instantly to retrieve the afghan that had fallen to the floor when she'd sat up. They were at odds somehow, in some way he didn't seem to want to explain at this point in time.

She wished she knew what it was.

"All I want for you," he said gently, pushing her back to the pillow and covering her again, "is for you to stay safe and deliver a healthy baby while remaining healthy yourself."

"And what do you want for you?" she asked.

He patted her cheek and then her tummy. "I've got it right here. Rest while I finish the dishes."

With his touch lingering on her, she closed her eyes, trying to remember what the obstacle was between them.

Whatever it was, she'd be willing to bet that it was a problem he had with her and not the other way around. She couldn't remember their past together, but she was falling in love all over again.

Chapter Three

Gusty stared at the small travel alarm on her night-stand. Illuminated green letters read 3:06 a.m. She was wide-awake.

She'd napped last night while Bram tidied the kitchen, then slept off and on while he replenished the fire and made notes in a leather folder he said held some of his detective agency's paperwork. She'd awakened an hour ago safely tucked in bed, and had been unable to fall asleep again.

She struggled out of bed, pulled on a flannel shirt Bram had given her to keep her warm during the cool evenings, then waddled quietly into the kitchen. She turned on the light over the stove, put the kettle on to boil, then pulled sandwich-makings out of the re-frigerator. She slathered cranberry sauce on bread, added chunky pieces of game hen and a generous portion of dressing. She had to push down on the sandwich to make sure it held together, then carried it into the living room.

She settled into the scratchy old upholstery of

Bram's chair and turned on the parchment-shade lamp on the table beside her. A little pool of light fell on her, the only bright space in the dark house.

It felt strange, she thought, to be all alone with herself when she didn't know who she was. So far, she'd defined herself by things Bram had told her, but certainly the true reality of a person could never be understood by someone else, even someone as close as a husband.

She imagined herself in a classroom talking to third-graders about wildflowers. She closed her eyes and tried to picture herself at a chalkboard, eager little faces watching her.

Leanne watching her.

Leanne with lots of blond hair but no face.

On her head was a cardboard crown with gold stars all over it. Gold stars. Gusty struggled to focus, wondering if the crown was something she remembered, or something her tired mind had simply put there.

Perhaps the crowns were a way she'd developed of scoring achievement. Maybe each star indicated something accomplished.

But she didn't know. She was only guessing. It might mean nothing at all.

In her mind, her eyes panned to the other children. Something reacted inside her. She felt happy. She liked children. She loved them.

She ran a hand over her baby and closed her eyes against her classroom, frustrated at her inability to remember.

But her baby was ever-present. She didn't have to

remember. Every day her belly swelled a little more as though trying to help her prove her own existence. *I'm here!* it seemed to say. *Even if I don't know who I am!*

The baby moved subtly as Gusty rubbed. She wished she could remember his conception. She was beginning to think of it as a boy because of his swift and sudden movements, his determination to keep her up nights with wild dancing, his tendency to push against her spinal column as he took up more and more space.

She wondered if he'd begun as the happy aftermath of a party, the warm afterglow of an intimate dinner or a spontaneous response to the passion in Bram's eyes—or his reaction to hers.

However it had happened, she thought, giving the baby another pat, she hoped he could be delivered in safety. The threat to her life seemed unreal—probably because she couldn't remember the incident that had prompted it—but when she considered the threat to her baby's life, the whole thing took on a terrifyingly real aspect.

Her sandwich half-finished, she put the plate aside and dropped her arm over the side of the chair, as she leaned back, trying to get comfortable. The baby seemed to resent her sending food down to take up his already cramped space. It felt as though he was stretching, feet braced against her spine, hands pushing at her ribs.

She stretched her legs out in an attempt to relieve

pressure and tried to flatten her back against the back of the chair, dropping her other arm over the side.

This was a mistake, she knew. It would take a crane to get her out of this chair when she was ready to go back to bed.

Her left hand encountered leather. She peered over the side of the chair and saw Bram's backpack tucked into the shadows between the small table and the chair. Thinking Bram might have misplaced it, she lifted it and leaned it against the front of the chair.

And as the pouch gaped when she caught it by the sides, she spotted what appeared to be the pencil-shaped antenna of a cell phone. She pulled the bag up into what was left of her lap and pulled out the instrument.

She stared at it in disbelief.

"We have no way to contact anyone unless we go to town," Bram had said when she'd asked how they would call for help if they needed it. "We could give away our location by making calls. So we have to depend upon ourselves."

No way to contact anyone and there'd been a cell phone in his backpack all along.

She looked deeper into the bag and saw a floral, very feminine looking address book. She pulled it out and opened it, guessing it was hers and not his. Or maybe one she kept for both of them.

She opened it and the first two names leaped out at her. Alexis Ames. Athena Ames.

She read them again, greedily searching for clues

to her sisters' personalities and possibly her own in the simple letters of their names.

Alexis had a European address and phone number, but Athena lived in Washington, D.C. Her eyes ran over the numbers.

"Interesting reading?" Bram asked. He stood in the living room doorway, long legs in sweat bottoms braced a foot apart, muscular arms crossed over a formidable chest clad in a simple white T-shirt.

"It's our address book," she said unnecessarily, to hide her guilt. Why did she feel guilty, she asked herself impatiently. She was rummaging through his things, but he'd been guilty of lying.

"Yes, it is," he said.

She held up the phone. "You told me we had no way to contact anyone," she accused, "unless we went to town."

He held her gaze intrepidly. "I didn't want you to try," he replied calmly. "I was afraid that if you started remembering things and tried to call your sisters or a friend, Mendez would track us down."

"You could have trusted me to understand that," she said with an air of injured dignity, "and to behave accordingly."

He raised a rueful eyebrow. "I might have if I didn't know you better. You have a tendency to do what you want to do regardless of the possible consequences."

"Then how do we get along," she asked, her chin at a testy angle, "if you don't trust me?"

He grinned. "I keep an eye on you." He indicated

the backpack with a jut of his chin. "You're welcome to dump everything out and look through it. I have nothing to hide."

"Except the phone you lied about."

He nodded with no apparent guilt. "Which you found by looking through my bag. I think that makes us even."

Indignant because he was right, she tried to pull herself out of the chair. She imagined she looked a little like a whale attempting a backbend.

Bram came to help her.

She tried to slap his hands away. "I can manage."

"Let me help you," he insisted. "I'm fond of that chair." Placing one hand on her arm and his other arm around her back, he pulled firmly and drew her to her feet.

"Thank you," she said with precarious dignity. "I'm going back to bed."

"Good idea." He walked her to her bedroom. "What woke you? Are you warm enough?"

"I was hungry," she admitted, rubbing her knuckles against the back of her waist. Or where she used to have a waist. "And the baby loves to stretch out when we sleep and push against my backbone."

She was walking into the room as she spoke, but Bram caught her arm and splayed his other hand against the small of her back. "Here?" he asked.

She felt several things at once—a little frisson of sensation that seemed to bounce from one vertebra to another, then the simple comfort of his broad, warm hand against her aching back.

"Yes," she replied, her voice barely there. She reached to the doorjamb for support as both the sensation and the warmth began to spread.

"Let me see if I can encourage him to move." He went to her bed, drawing her with him, and sat down on the edge. He patted his knee, encouraging her to sit on it.

She eyed him skeptically, concerned on several levels. She could explain only one. "I'll cripple you," she warned.

He laughed. "I don't think so. I've been running five miles a day for twenty years." He pulled her between his legs and sat her on his right knee. "And there's not that much to you, even with the baby." He placed his hand over the spot she'd indicated before and rubbed gently but firmly.

She pitched forward at the strength of the first stroke and he put his free arm around her to anchor her.

In a matter of seconds she became his willing slave. She couldn't help the "aah" of relief as his left arm supported her uncomfortable weight and his right hand rubbed that pressure point until she felt like a puddle of oatmeal.

"Better?" she heard Bram ask.

She considered answering no, because if she said yes, he'd stop.

Reluctantly she made an affirmative sound and pushed herself to her feet. "Thank you," she whispered, the air suddenly electric around them. They should be sharing a bed, a life, a baby. But there were too many unknowns here for her to settle comfortably into life as it should be.

All she knew about herself was what he'd told her—and if he'd lied about the phone, he might have lied about anything else—or everything else.

He stood, also, and gestured her into bed. "I'll tuck you in," he offered.

She complied and he lifted her feet for her, pulling the blankets over them, then over her.

She lay on her side, the only position that was comfortable, and he tucked the blankets in at her neck.

He turned out the light. "Sweet dreams," he said into the darkness.

"Thank you for the massage," she replied.

"All part of the service."

The door closed quietly and she expelled a deep sigh of relief. When she knew who she was, she wondered, would she know what to make of him?

BRAM WAS ALMOST GLAD to see rain the following morning. It was cold and damp and they went through a lot of wood, giving him something to do that afternoon.

He chopped enough wood to replace the power of Bonneville Dam. He was frustrated on so many levels he was about to implode. But he had to bide his time.

In his other life, the government had directed him to a point, but he'd been the best security officer they had and they'd let him do things his way.

When he'd hooked up with Dave and Trev, they'd worked together like a well-maintained machine, each moving in harmony with the other, each mind reading the others' so that there was seldom a bad move.

Until Afghanistan and Farah's death.

Bram remembered explaining to them why they shouldn't use her, that while she was valuable as a translator, she was outside the unit and therefore a potential danger.

But they'd needed her, and he'd fallen under the spell of her intelligence and her sweetness just like Dave had—though neither of them had fallen as hard or as far as Trevyn.

When they'd closed in on Raisu to stop his terrorism of American installations all over the world, Trev had told her to stay behind. But she'd had some scheme about distracting the camp so that the three of them could approach unnoticed, and she'd ignored Trevyn, determined to do what she thought would help.

He remembered hearing her scream when her traitorous brother had mistaken her for them and shot her. Then he remembered seeing her lying there, arms flung out and motionless.

Bram cleaved a wide log of cedar in half with a clean stroke of the ax as he remembered Trevyn's primal scream.

The mission gone bad, they had no choice but to retreat. Trevyn wouldn't leave without Farah's body, and Bram covered their escape while Dave helped Trev carry her down the mountain.

They'd decided to quit after that, each weary of the business for his own reasons. Staying together in civilian life, at least until they'd all found another road, seemed like the sensible thing to do.

Then David had inherited the house in Dancer's Beach from their CIA radio contact, code-named "Auntie." He'd saved her life during an African uprising, and in gratitude, she'd left him her home.

That was where Bram had first met Gusty at a costume party. He and his friends had been dressed as the Three Musketeers, and Gusty had worn a velvet bonnet and a dress with petticoats and she'd caught his eye right away.

He'd excused himself from the group he'd been talking with and taken her aside so they could talk.

She hadn't wanted to talk about herself, had tried instead to make him talk about the house, about how they'd come by it and which one of them owned it.

He'd told her about his sister, his nieces, his years looking for something to validate his existence. With a father who was a felon, and an alcoholic mother, he'd grown up wondering how he could be of any value.

Only his younger sister's dependence upon him had forced him to try, and her gratitude and her reliance on him finally taught him that they were both better than the genes that made them up.

He'd joined the police force when she'd gotten married at sixteen and developed into just the kind of young man who could fit into the military. He had what it took, he could rise above, learn that adversity could strengthen and not destroy if a man was determined to be a winner.

And that was when Gusty had opened up a little about herself, though he'd learned later that it hadn't all been the truth.

She'd told him she was a teacher, and that she lived in northern California in a small town called Pansy Junction, but she hadn't mentioned her sisters. She'd told him she was visiting friends in Dancer's Beach.

She was always trying to find her place, too, she'd said. That she had a tendency to be cowardly, to avoid risk and danger and heartbreak.

He'd pointed out that dealing with children every day seemed very brave to him.

Then she'd smiled and he'd seen something final in her eyes.

He'd pulled her toward him and kissed her, then he'd lifted her mask and looked into the sweetest face he'd ever seen.

She'd looked back at him with undisguised longing, then run off when Mayor Beasley had come in search of him to introduce him to a guest.

He'd run after her as soon as he'd been able to get free, but there had been a storm outside and there'd been no sign of her.

He'd had a surveillance job the following day, and during the long, tedious hours of waiting and watching, he'd called Information for Pansy Junction, California, and gotten the telephone number for the school.

With that, it had been a simple thing to check the roster of teachers at the Pansy Junction Elementary School, then to call Information again with her name.

He'd gotten her telephone number and her address but knew he'd get nowhere calling her. So he'd hopped a plane the following weekend.

She'd been working on flower boxes and, when she'd turned to watch him climb out of his rental car, he'd seen both delight and surprise in her eyes.

And then she'd run into his arms.

As his closed around her, he'd known that she was what his life was supposed to be about, that his search was over.

And somehow, over the intervening eight months, that delicious discovery had turned into this desperate hiding out from the man who wanted to take it all away from him.

GUSTY LISTENED to the rhythmic strikes of Bram's ax and felt as though she would cheerfully give up a year of her life if she could remember just a minute of her life with Bram before she'd surfaced in the river. It was becoming as important to her to know who *he* was as to know herself.

He was her husband, and the baby tied them to each other inextricably, but was he the caring, gentle person he seemed to be? Or had she glimpsed something else last night when he'd caught her going through his backpack?

He hadn't shouted or accused, but she was sure she'd detected anger. Because she'd been snooping, she wondered, or because she'd caught him in a lie?

The uncertainty put her on edge.

Her back aching from a morning spent baking cinnamon bread, she went into the bedroom, intent on lying down for a few minutes. Then she saw herself in the three-way mirror on the old-fashioned vanity near her bed.

She groaned as she approached the mirror and sat down on the small stool. She looked like an obese bag lady, complete with big, loose dress topped with the flannel shirt. She'd braided her hair to keep it out of her face while she was cooking, but she'd done it quickly because she'd overslept, and now she looked disheveled and pathetic, like Pippi Longstocking on a bender.

Pippi Longstocking. Was that knowledge or memory? She was tired of asking herself that question.

Quickly she unbraided her hair and ran a brush through it, determined to pile it up into a tidy knot. This afternoon she wanted to clean kitchen cupboards. She felt both exhausted and frenzied, as though she was too tired to do anything, but had to or die.

She was drawing the brush from the crown of her hair through the long, rippled mass to the ends when she caught her triple reflection and felt something akin to a lightning strike right between her eyes.

Crack! Sizzle! Truth! Triplets. She was a triplet. Bram had told her that. She'd known it, but she hadn't understood, hadn't *remembered* it until this moment.

She was Gusty Ames. Triplet! And the other two images she saw were Lexie and Athena. But in her mind, she couldn't see them as adults. All she could remember were three little girls peering into this mirror, pouting, crying.

Why?

"Disneyland!" Lexie said. She threw something. Gusty could see it flying but couldn't tell what it had been.

She remembered suddenly that they'd been promised a trip to Disneyland but something in their parents' schedule had changed and they took off for some other destination without them and left them with Aunt…Aunt…Sadie! Aunt Sadie!

Excited by the memories, Gusty pursued them, trying to remember more.

And as her mind chased those few details, it was as though a mist fell between her and them, closing them off.

She wanted to throw something but forced herself to calm down. She'd been warned this would be a slow and unpredictable process. She had to be patient.

Briskly she brushed her hair and wound it into a loose knot. She pulled out a few tendrils at her ears and her temple, then studied her reflection in surprise.

Why had she done that? Was that memory or habit? At least it was a new variation on the old question.

Momentarily tired of that worry, she brushed the sides up tidily, retied the knot and looked in her closet for something more stylish to wear.

But there was nothing. Bram said she'd lost everything she'd had with her when the rental car sank with her luggage. They'd left home quickly after the mysterious calls and she'd brought only the clothes on her back—this dress. He had bought her a few things—the overalls she wore all the time because they were comfortable, and a pair of black maternity slacks and a big white sweater that hung in the closet beside the overalls.

That was it.

And for reasons she couldn't explain, that made her dissolve into tears.

She ripped off the offending flannel shirt and the dress.

GUSTY WAS STANDING in front of her closet in a long slip and a very no-nonsense white cotton bra when Bram found her. He'd stacked the wood and had gone looking for a cup of coffee when he'd seen the pot was empty and she wasn't in the kitchen cooking or in the living room, working on the baby sweater she was knitting.

"What?" she demanded, crossing her arms over her chest. Her large belly rested under her breasts like some globular support. She looked tearful and cross. "What do you want?"

He advanced into the room with some trepidation. She was the dearest woman he'd ever known, but she had a temper to rival his own when it was aroused. What had done it this afternoon?

"A cup of coffee," he said carefully. "But the pot's empty. What's the matter?"

"Just because I *can* cook," she said angrily, snatching up his old flannel shirt off the bed, "It doesn't mean I *have* to, does it? I mean, you're perfectly capable of making coffee!" She jammed an arm into a sleeve.

"I didn't mean you had to make it. I just…"

"You just wondered why I hadn't!" One sleeve on, she reached behind herself for the other, growing testier as it eluded her. "Well, maybe I didn't feel like cooking! Maybe, if we're going to be stuck out here for all eternity, I'm giving some thought to spinning yarn and weaving cloth and making myself something to…damn it! Where the hell is the…"

Knowing he was risking life and limb, he came behind her, put her arm into the sleeve and danced back quickly as she rounded on him, yanking the fronts of the shirt together. Or trying to. They gaped over the baby.

That made her cry.

He shifted his weight and analyzed the situation, knowing touching her wouldn't be safe. This was new territory for him. He'd faced her temper before, but not without a valid reason behind it. He had to find out what the problem was.

"Gus?" he asked reasonably.

"I don't want to be Gus!" she snarled at him, then stomped out of the bedroom and into the living room, where she didn't seem to be able to decide where to go from there. She turned in circles.

He stood aside and waited.

"I don't want to be huge and ugly and completely unfamiliar to myself."

"You're not unfamiliar to me," he put in quietly.

That didn't help. "Well, *you're* unfamiliar to me!" she shouted back tearfully. "I don't know my own husband! Can you have any idea what that feels like?'' She put a hand to her stomach, her voice quieting a decibel. "I don't remember making this baby. If I could, it might make up in some way for the fact that I look like a polar bear with a red wig! A polar bear with nothing to wear!''

Well, now he knew what the problems were—and there were several of them—but he couldn't do anything about most of them.

He concentrated on the one for which he had a solution.

"He was conceived after we went dancing,'' he said. She'd stopped at the window looking out onto the rainy meadow, an amusing picture in tennis shoes, a long slip, and a flannel shirt that didn't close. "We'd had a little champagne and the orchestra played a tango.''

She turned to him in surprise. "We can tango?''

He grinned. "No, we can't. And we proved it that night. We were at the American Legion dance in the Baptist church's community hall and ended up in a very undignified pile at the foot of the stage.''

She winced. "What happened?''

He shrugged. "As I recall, it was a physics problem. I had swung you out and was reeling you back in when you tripped, crashed against me and we both went down.''

"Did they throw us out?''

"No, they applauded. I think they appreciated our guts. Or our stupidity. I'm not sure which.''

Her smile crumpled suddenly and a tear fell. "I wonder what happened to my guts,'' she asked plaintively. "I'm scared and tired and..." She lost her last shred of composure. "Really, really fat!"

He wrapped her in his arms, half-expecting her to resist, but she stood docilely against him, weeping as he rubbed her back.

"You're not fat, you're pregnant," he corrected, "and you've shown a lot of guts through this whole thing. Of course you're tired and scared. Think about what you've been through—half-drowned, dragged off into hiding by a man you don't remember who makes you bake him cookies and make coffee..."

She looked into his face suddenly, her eyes large and tear filled, her arms looped around his neck, and asked, "So we made love to celebrate how silly we looked at the dance?"

"No." He smoothed her hair and resisted the urge to kiss her senseless. "We made love because we're very passionate about each other. You thought the tango would be fun. I was a little reluctant, but because you wanted to try, I did it. I think you were rewarding me for my support, and I was encouraging your sense of adventure."

She gave him a small smile. "So maybe our son should have an Argentinean name if he was conceived as the result of a tango."

"Fernando, or something?"

She thought. "Or Enrique. Trevyn Enrique Bishop. How does that sound?"

"Confused, but who cares?"

She lay her head on his shoulder and her weight

against him and heaved a deep sigh. He held her, valuing the moment.

"What did I wear when we went dancing?" she asked.

"Ah…" He scrambled to think. "A dark blue sparkly thing with a short, ruffly skirt. You were gorgeous."

She sighed again. "You think it'll still fit me after I have the baby?"

"Yes, I do."

She raised her head to look into his face, her expression filled with dark amusement. "That was the right answer, but you're lying. I feel as though I'm carrying forty extra pounds, and when the baby's born, he'll only weigh seven or eight."

He shook his head. "Your pre-pregnancy weight is 126. You weigh 153 now."

"That's—" she narrowed an eye as she calculated "—thirty-seven pounds!"

"No," he corrected patiently. "It's twenty-seven pounds. I hope you use a calculator in class."

"Oh." She seemed more relieved by the truth than upset by her mistake. "But I still look like a humvee."

"Come on." He put an arm around her shoulders and led her back to the bedroom. "Put something on and we'll go find you something to wear that makes you happy, then we'll have dinner somewhere."

She resisted at the door to the bedroom. "I'd love to have dinner, but Paintbrush is so small, the Mercantile won't have maternity clothes."

"We'll try anyway." He peeled her fingers from the molding and pushed her gently inside. "I'll be ready in fifteen minutes."

"It'll take me a year and half!" she called to him.

"I'll wait!" he called back.

Chapter Four

Gusty was delighted to discover that she'd been wrong. The Mathews Mercantile, the only shop that sold clothing in downtown Paintbrush, had four maternity outfits crowded in among work shirts, jeans and barn coats.

There was a black-and-white-check jumper with a tailored white cotton shirt, several pairs of stretch leggings in various colors, several hooded sweatshirts and a bright red sweater with a turtleneck.

The proprietor, a cheerful man in his late thirties, attributed their stock to the fact that his wife was now pregnant with their fourth child.

Gusty pulled the jumper off the rack and held it up in front of herself in the mirror. "This looks teachery, doesn't it?" she asked Bram.

He was examining a blue barn coat with red trim and brought it with him as he came to stand behind her and study her reflection.

"Maybe," he said tactfully, "but not your usual taste."

She held his gaze in the mirror, interested. "What is my usual taste?"

"Ah…silky, floaty, very feminine stuff."

She looked at herself, trying to superimpose that style on the large woman in the mirror. She sighed. "Well, there isn't anything like that here, and I'm not exactly a romantic figure at the moment."

"I beg to differ," he said, taking the jumper from her and giving her the coat to hold. He hung up the jumper and looked through the small collection of maternity things. "To the man whose baby you're carrying, you're a very romantic figure. Bosomy and with a round belly, you're the classic fertility image, the earth mother who used to run the world in prehistory." He pulled out three pairs of leggings, two hooded sweatshirts in colors to coordinate with the pants and the red sweater. "What about these? They might not be what you'd choose, but you'll make them look romantic."

She was flattered by his assessment, but somewhere deep down, unable to believe he was real.

"And I guess I'm lucky to find anything," she said.

"True. And try the coat on. Your jacket's not going to do it when it starts snowing."

It was a fingertip-length jacket in a much larger size than she wore, but it did button. The neck gaped because of the size, and he yanked a wooly red plaid scarf off a rack and wrapped it twice around her throat.

She would never make the cover of *W*, but she would be warm.

She changed into the graphite leggings and the red sweater while Bram paid for the purchases. She brushed her hair into order and caught it into a high ponytail with the simple dark hair elastic that seemed to be all she had to keep it in order besides a few pins.

She looked a little more lively than she had earlier, she thought, attributing that to the color of the sweater. Redheads were not supposed to wear certain colors, but she'd never abided by...that.

She'd never abided by that! How did she know? Because she'd *remembered* it!

"Bram!" she shouted, coming out of the small closetlike dressing room to find Bram standing right there with their packages, waiting for her. "I remembered something else!"

Had she detected the smallest hint of worry in his eyes just before he smiled? She couldn't be sure but dismissed the notion, caught up in her own excitement.

"I wear red and all kinds of other colors redheads are warned away from!"

He didn't seem to find that justification for her excitement. "Really," he said.

"Don't you see?" she demanded. "I remembered something about me! Something you didn't have to tell me! I wear red! I'm a...a fashion maverick!" She gave that a little thought, then added uncertainly, "Or a fashion disaster, maybe."

The man behind the counter laughed. "Brace yourself, sir. The last month of pregnancy is a minefield of mood swings. Just let her have her way. Once the baby comes, she won't belong to you anymore.''

Feeling lighthearted, Gusty blew the proprietor a kiss as she and Bram walked out the door. "That was good advice," she said gravely. "Let me have my way in all things and we'll be very happy."

"Well, what is it you want?" He unlocked the car door and tossed the bundles inside. "You never ask for anything."

She raised an eyebrow as he locked and closed the door. "Well, I'm obviously suffering from some misguided sense of selflessness. Thank goodness, we've caught it in time. I want a big steak and strawberry shortcake."

He took hold of her elbow, waited for a pickup loaded with fence posts to pass, then walked with her across the street to the Paintbrush Diner. "It's October, Gus. Strawberries are out of season."

"Well, there must be frozen ones somewhere." She squeezed his arm, feeling happy. It was a new experience since her dunk in the Columbia. "Honestly," she taunted, "I hope you're not so easily put off by every little obstacle."

IF SHE ONLY KNEW, Bram thought. But she didn't, and right now, that was best.

They had steaks, waffle fries and green beans with bacon. He watched Gusty in her flattering red sweater and youthful ponytail eat with more than her usual enthusiasm.

"Tell me," he teased. "Gusty stands for Gusto, rather than Augusta, doesn't it?"

She looked at him blankly for a moment, then laughed in embarrassment. "Am I scarfing? I'm sorry. I'm just feeling more—I don't know—hopeful, I guess. It makes me hungry."

"Good. I'm sure the rest of your pregnancy will take a lot of energy." He hoped desperately that this would be over and he could get her out of here before she was ready to deliver. There was a very small hospital in Paintbrush, but he doubted they'd be equipped to handle problems. And there was a possibility there could be some. He was grateful she didn't remember that.

"Am I your first marriage?" she asked abruptly, putting steak sauce on her last bite of steak. She added another little dollop to the side and dipped a waffle fry in it.

"Yes," he replied. "But I'm your fourth husband, I believe."

She stopped with a fry halfway to her mouth, her eyes widening in astonishment.

"There was a radical activist when you were in college," he said, leaning back as a waitress poured more coffee into their cups. He continued with a straight face, "a stockbroker when you were twenty-three and that Italian prince you met at Le Mans."

"You're kidding!" she gasped, her face pale with horror.

"Yeah, I am," he admitted, laughing as she aimed

a punch at his shoulder. "I just wanted to see how entrenched this sudden good humor is."

She punched him again. "Lucky for you, it's solid. Now. Let's go find some strawberries."

Fortunately, the tiny Paintbrush deli had a bag of strawberries in the freezer, and a can of whipped cream.

"Don't we need those sponge cake cups?" he asked as she placed their shortcake ingredients on the counter.

"I can make biscuits," she said. "And don't think you're getting any after that fourth-husband fib."

"You just said your good humor was solid."

"Maybe *I* fibbed."

But it was solid. After they reached the house, she sang what seemed to be some child's song about birds and butterflies while she whipped up biscuits and dropped them onto a cookie sheet.

"Just quick biscuits," she said, wiping her hands on her apron, "but I like those best for shortcake anyway." She smiled suddenly, aware that was another discovery about herself.

Across the small kitchen, he planed a sticking drawer and forced himself to remain calm. There was no need to panic. Things were going somewhat according to plan. There was every reason to believe they would work out in his favor. Every reason.

"I like strawberries on waffles," he said, sliding the drawer in and out. It still dragged a little. He planed again.

"There'll be half a bag left," she said as she put

the sheet of biscuits into the oven. "There's a waffle iron in that corner cupboard."

"You *do* make good waffles."

She grinned. "If you're my fourth husband, I've had lots of practice. You claim to have married me for my cookies, but I'll bet it was for my alimony."

He frowned and tried the drawer again. "I don't think your exes have to pay when you're remarried. Child support continues, but not the alimony."

"Heck of a deal. Have we talked about whether or not I'll work after the baby comes?"

Satisfied with the drawer, he touched it up with sandpaper. "We argued about that a little. You want to take the standard maternity leave, and I'd prefer you stayed home. At least for the first year."

She wiped off the counter and stopped, apparently analyzing her feelings. "That's funny. I don't feel as though I'd want to go back—at least for a while. Maybe this school year."

She met his gaze, as though waiting for his thoughts on her observation.

"You did say this experience was making you feel differently." He wiped off the sides and the bottom of the drawer with a damp cloth. "Maybe you're just changing your mind. A perfectly acceptable reaction to different circumstances."

She shook her head, apparently concerned. "This is weird. Not only do I not know who I am, but I'm turning into someone different from that. How will I even know who I am if I'm no longer the same person?"

Bram wrapped his arms around her, trying to intercept the worried mood that had brought her to tears earlier. "You analyze too deeply, Gus," he said, giving her and therefore the baby, a little squeeze. "You're very together. You'll know yourself, even if you've evolved into someone new."

She looked up at him, a curious distance in her eyes he didn't feel at all. Then he remembered that she didn't remember their relationship. God. This was like a puzzle with too many missing pieces to create a picture.

"What about you?" she asked gravely. "You married the woman I was. What if I turn into someone you can't love in the same way?"

He did have an answer for that. "That couldn't happen," he assured her. "You're grafted on to me. We're growing together into something new. Nothing can affect that."

"Is it safe to be so sure of things?" she asked with a wry smile.

He shrugged. "Nothing's safe, and nothing's sure. So I can think as I please."

Something warmed in her eyes and closed the distance he'd seen there. "I suppose I fell in love with you because you have all the answers."

He grinned. "You said it was because you liked my butt in jogging shorts."

She rolled her eyes. "Did I really say that?"

"Even during the wedding ceremony."

"What?"

"When the minister asked you, 'Do you take this

man' and so on, you said, 'I do, because he has the cutest…'"

He was interrupted by the oven timer. She swatted his arm with a pot holder, then pulled out the biscuits while he replaced the tool in the garage and washed his hands.

BRAM STOKED UP THE FIRE and they ate the shortcake on the sofa facing the fireplace. It had started to rain again, and it beat against the roof and windows, making their warm little haven seem safe and secure.

He told her about one of his cases, and as she listened to the deep, comforting timbre of his voice she found it hard to believe that anything existed beyond this room, much less anything threatening.

They went to their separate beds shortly after ten o'clock and Gusty went right to sleep.

She awoke again at 2:17, knowing instantly what had jarred her out of sleep. The baby was exercising again—feet against her spine, arms pushing out against her ribs. She could just imagine him standing on his head and kicking at her lumbar vertebrae, doing tricks in the gym of her womb. She hoped that didn't mean he was showing off for a twin the ultrasound had missed!

She pulled the flannel shirt on over her nightgown and padded out to the kitchen as she'd done the night before. She doubted she'd be lucky enough a second time for Bram to hear her and apply the massage that had finally relieved her discomfort last night.

She wasn't in the mood for a turkey sandwich and

reached for the plastic-wrapped plate of biscuits, then decided that was too heavy for the hour and would only exaggerate her problem.

She finally decided on a glass of milk. She put it in a pan to warm it, then poured it into a mug and carried it out to the living room. She sat in Bram's chair again but left the room dark this time. She dropped a hand over the side of the chair, wondering if she would encounter his backpack.

She didn't. He must have taken it into his room with him.

And that was fine. His arguments about why he hadn't told her about the phone were very logical, though they'd offended her last night. They couldn't risk discovery. She understood that.

But she wondered what her sisters were doing. She still couldn't see them as adults, though she knew they looked just like she did. She could only remember the three of them as children, quarreling over something but allied in their common cause against their mother.

It was odd, she thought, that she remembered that but couldn't bring her face into focus, or the faces of her sisters, or her father.

She could remember what she'd felt—sad, hurt, even betrayed. It was a strong feeling—as though she'd lived with it a long time. Into adulthood, probably.

Her sisters must have coped well if Alexis was an artist and Athena a lawyer. They'd been stronger than she as children; she was sure of that. She'd felt inferior. She could feel it now.

Did they miss her, she wondered, or did they consider themselves well rid of her? Perhaps she'd been of little value to them as an adult.

Was someone missing Bram? Were David and Trevyn wondering where he was? He'd told her they were accustomed to his long absences on cases that led out of town or into long surveillances.

But three weeks? Certainly someone was searching for them besides the man who wanted to kill them.

Bram's door opened suddenly. She waited for the sound of footsteps but heard nothing. She opened her mouth to call his name, but he called hers first.

"Augusta!"

It was a swift, sharp shout with an edge of anger in it.

The reverberating sound parted a curtain in her mind and, though the image remained clouded, she heard the sound again from somewhere in the past. "Augusta!" Her full name shouted in what sounded like panic—angry panic.

She wanted to answer, but she couldn't. Her heartbeat accelerated and her mouth went dry as she struggled to remember what had happened when Bram had last spoken to her in such a tone.

She was shaking inside, felt cornered, pursued.

"Augusta!" said the voice from the past again. "The baby is mine, and you're not walking away from me!"

The threat was clear.

They'd been fighting over the baby. She sat frozen in the darkness in the chair, struggling to remember why.

"You're not walking away from me!" he had said. Had she been trying to leave him? What had he done?

She couldn't remember, but she knew her sense of unease, of something wrong between them had been right from the beginning.

"Gusty!"

A light went on in the cabin's living room, and her brief glimpse into the past disappeared. The fear and the internal tremors, however, stayed with her.

Bram strode across the room toward her, barefoot and wearing sweatpants and T-shirt. He also wore a dark frown and an air of annoyance.

"Why didn't you answer me?" he demanded, crouching down before her. "You scared the hell out of me!"

Calm, she told herself. *Just be calm. He can't read your mind.*

She smiled and held up her milk mug in one trembling hand. "Couldn't sleep again. I thought some milk would help me. Did you call me? I must have dozed off in the dark."

His frown deepened as he leaned down to pull her out of the chair. Her heart lurched against her ribs. "I thought I heard you in the kitchen, then I got up to check on you and the place is pitch-black. I thought we had an intruder or something. Then, when you didn't answer..."

"I'm sorry," she said quickly. "Last night the light

woke you, and I thought one of us should get some sleep.''

''The fire's out and you're trembling,'' he scolded, rubbing his hands up and down her arms. His eyes softened suddenly and he asked in a quieter voice, ''The baby's on your spine again?''

Bram walked her to his bedroom. ''You want to give yourself pneumonia? Why didn't you wrap up in a blanket?'' Without waiting for an answer, he put her into his bed, still warm from his body, covered her, then pushed her onto her side so that he could reach under the blankets and massage her back.

She didn't understand how the action could seem erotic when she was suddenly unsure of who he was and what they were doing here together. The bed smelled of his herbal aftershave and the wood he spent so much time chopping.

Was she really in danger from some outside source, or had he simply taken her into hiding—away from family and friends—so that she could deliver their baby with no one else around, allowing him to keep it? That was certainly the surefire way to prevent her from leaving him, and that had apparently been her intention at one point.

She couldn't remember the details, but his shout of her name had brought back that part of their conversation very clearly.

But she had fallen into the Columbia River. She remembered surfacing and she still had the remnants of a bruise. She touched her forehead as she thought about it.

Something inside her jolted at a new thought.

Had Bram bumped her car into the river?

Maybe he'd originally intended to punish her for leaving him, then, when she survived, but with amnesia, realized that if he hid her out somewhere until she delivered the baby, he could still get what he wanted.

Maybe that was why he hadn't told her about the phone.

The phone. She had to be careful, but she had to find the phone.

"You're still shaking," Bram said. "You warming up?"

"Yes, thank you," she said. Her voice sounded unconvincing. Though she felt she appeared calm, she seemed powerless to stop the tremor inside that had begun with his shout of her name.

"The baby still stretching?" he asked.

"I think he's gone to sleep." She tried to relax her muscles so that his hands would interpret that as comfort restored and he would let her go back to her own bed.

Apparently she failed.

"You still feel cold and tense," he said, turning off the bedside light. "Scoot over a little, Gus. I think you'd better stay here with me tonight and let me keep you warm."

"That's not..." she began to argue. Then he was beside her, his arm coming around her to tuck her into the reclinerlike curve of his body. His warmth permeated her chill despite her fears. The baby, and therefore her body, began to relax.

With his arm around her, he tugged on her gently. "Let yourself relax against me. Even if the baby insists on riding your spine, you won't have to bear the weight."

One arm under her, providing a pillow for her head, the other holding her in her deliciously comfortable position, Bram said simply, "Good night, Gus."

She experienced about ninety seconds of confounding confusion over her attempt to understand this man and his intentions, then fell fast asleep.

IT WAS EASIER than Gusty thought to find the phone.

Bram climbed atop the woodshed roof to repair a hole he'd discovered before breakfast. Gusty took advantage of his absence to search his room. She found the backpack in his closet, but no cell phone or address book.

She checked the dresser then his nightstand, and found the phone tucked in behind several boxes of ammunition. But she couldn't locate the address book.

He'd apparently made less effort hiding the phone, thinking he had to keep it handy on the chance he needed it. But he must have thought that while she might locate the phone, she could do nothing damaging with it if she couldn't find the address book to make calls.

But he hadn't counted on a teacher's skill for memorization. Years of lesson plans and lists of things one had to memorize in order to teach children to do the same had honed her skill to an art form.

She remembered Athena's office phone number though she'd seen it for only seconds two days ago.

She went into the bathroom, locked the door and dialed the number.

A kind but confident voice said, "You've reached the former office of Athena Ames, Attorney-at-Law. Because of marriage and a new family, I've moved my office from Washington, D.C., to Dancer's Beach, Oregon. If you're calling about a new case, the following attorneys are dividing my local caseload." She listed several names and numbers. "If you're interested in reaching me in Dancer's Beach, I'm now Athena Hartford, and that telephone number is..." She listed the number. "Thank you for your call."

Her sister had gotten married since Gusty had been missing? She must have, because Bram thought she still lived in D.C., and she'd said she'd moved to Oregon because of her marriage and new family.

Hartford? Where had she heard that name before. And Dancer's Beach? She couldn't ask Bram or he'd guess she'd made the call.

Dear God. Had she just made an already impossible situation even more impossible to understand? Apart from leaving her feeling miserably disappointed that she hadn't reached Athena, she now felt more at a loss than ever.

"Gusty!" Bram's voice shouted from beyond the door.

She turned on the water faucet and pitched the telephone into the clothes hamper. She was the only one who did laundry. "Just washing my hands!" she shouted back.

"You okay?"

"Fine!"

When she walked into the kitchen, he was warming chili for lunch. "The roof patch isn't beautiful," he said, giving the contents a stir with a wooden spoon. "But it'll keep our wood dry. You look a little peaked. Your back still hurt?"

"No, I'm fine." She reached into the refrigerator for onions and cheese. "Thanks for making breakfast this morning. I haven't slept that well since...well, since I don't remember when."

"Good," he said, smiling at her as she went to work slicing onions and grating cheese on a cutting board near the stove. "You should probably let me cook from now on. Standing in one place will only get harder on your back as time goes on. Meals won't be as exciting, but we'll survive."

"No, then you'd have to cook *and* patch the roof, chop wood, and all the other things you do. I just have to remember to sit down to peel potatoes, chop onions, that sort of thing."

He pulled a chair out for her at the kitchen table and moved her chopping board and its contents. "There. When you're finished with that, I'll bring you the salad stuff."

"Okay. And there's the leftover strawberry short-cake for dessert."

The rain had stopped and a strong autumn sun

shone through the living room's small-paned windows. The worn fabric on the furniture looked bright and new and a few brass ornaments on the mantel glinted as though polished.

Bram stood at the stove, neat hips and long legs well defined in old jeans, the broadness of his back exaggerated by the close fit of the old knit military sweater across it.

Despite its few incongruities, the scene was cozily domestic. They did get along well most of the time, so why had she been so determined to leave him?

She wondered if he'd been more in the habit of displaying the anger she remembered from that argument about her leaving. He was always patient and considerate now, but perhaps that was so that she *wouldn't* remember his temper.

She sighed as she finished grating a mound of cheese. While that was possible, she really didn't think it was the answer. It was difficult to believe that a man prone to displays of temper could sustain the pretense of good humor over three weeks' time of being confined with a woman whose emotions varied widely from one moment to the next.

Still something had definitely been wrong. She remembered the heat of that argument, the anguish she'd felt.

At the first possible moment, she would call the Dancer's Beach number. She reminded herself that she had to put the phone back where he kept it before he noticed it was missing.

She found an opportunity to do so after lunch when Bram went to bring in more wood.

"I'm going to do a load of laundry," she said casually. "Anything you want to add that isn't in the hamper?"

He shook his head. "You've conditioned me to be tidy."

The moment the door closed behind him, she went into the bathroom to gather up their few things in one armful and plunged her free hand into the middle for the phone. She made a few false stabs and her heart was pounding when she finally found it.

She hurried into his bedroom, dropped the phone into his bedside table drawer and turned to leave. And felt the breath whoosh out of her lungs.

Bram stood in the open doorway, a shoulder leaning against the jamb. But despite the pose, he wasn't entirely relaxed. She'd seen that look on him before when they went to town, or whenever he'd heard an unfamiliar noise. He was alert to something that made him suspicious.

Her.

"You beginning to like it in here?" he asked. The question was spoken lightly, but there was a clear challenge in his eyes.

With a quick smile for him, she pointed to the floor on her side of the bed where a piece of white cotton protruded from under the bed.

"I remembered seeing a sock in here this morning when I got up, so I came to add it to the load." She laughed with convincing, self-deprecating humor.

"But I can't bend to get it. I was about to give up. Can you get it for me?"

He studied her for one protracted moment and, just when she expected him to tell her she was lying, he straightened and came around the bed to pick up the sock.

Only it wasn't a sock. It was panties. She had yet to get dressed this morning and somehow hadn't noticed that she was without them.

He dropped them into the bundle in her arms and patted her shoulder. "Don't look so horrified. You were restless during the night and pulling at the waistband through your nightie, as though they were making you uncomfortable. So I took them off you. Why did you wear them to sleep, anyway?"

She thought about that and realized she didn't know. "Habit, I guess."

He shook his head. "No habit that I recall."

She felt color rising into her cheeks and a fluster chipping away at her composure. "Well, I told you a lot of things are changing about me." And she tried to walk around him.

He caught her arm, his eyes filled with amusement. She stared him down, determined to survive this without complete humiliation.

"You're going to tell me that's a change you're not in favor of?" she asked.

He shrugged a shoulder. "They're easily removed, so it doesn't matter. I was coming to tell you that I noticed your skin's very dry and I have some cream that might help. I use it on my hands."

She opened her mouth to reply but couldn't think of a thing to say. What on earth was the problem between them? she wondered. He was caring to a fault.

"Gus," he said with mild impatience. He apparently interpreted her confused expression as dismay. "I'm your husband. But I'm not in the habit of taking you in your sleep, so relax."

"I didn't think you were," she replied, also impatient. "I just don't remember our intimacies, so this is all a little difficult for me."

"I know, I know. But you slept in my arms last night as though your subconscious remembers. And that knocked down the barriers I'd put up to stop myself from acting like your husband. So when you look at me as though I'm some stranger taking advantage—"

"I'm sorry," she interrupted with a sigh. "Really, Bram. I'm sorry. I'm grateful for all you've done, I just wish we could either get out of here, or that my memory would come back so that I'd understand us better."

He smiled dryly. "That might not happen even when you start remembering." He scooped the laundry out of her arms and led the way toward the small mudroom at the back that held the washer and dryer. "I said we were in love, but I didn't say we understood each other."

Chapter Five

Something was going on with Gusty, Bram was sure. But he didn't want to ask for fear she'd tell him she'd remembered something. Maybe even everything. He'd spent weeks wondering what he'd do in that eventuality and he was no closer to an answer.

But it was going to happen any day now. He had to have answers. A lot of them.

He stood on the porch looking out at the sunset, neon pink and purple as the sun went down behind the mountains. All he knew for certain was that he wasn't going to lose her. How he would make her accept that, he had no idea.

The door opened behind him and her voice said amiably if a little tightly, "Dinner's ready."

It had been an awkward afternoon, sexual tension strong between them since the panty incident, and though she'd done her best to behave normally, he knew it had been a strain.

If Mendez would show himself, he'd cheerfully

murder him for all he'd put the two of them through.
Still, if it hadn't been for him, she'd have left by now.

He held his place at the top of the stairs, but
reached an arm out to her to draw her against him.
She came without complaint.

"You're a real fan of sunsets," he said, pointing
to the blazing horizon. "Your dream is that one day
we'll watch one on the deck of a cruise ship headed
for the Mediterranean."

"Mmm," she said dreamily, "The Mediterranean."

"I think the plan was that we could visit Alexis on
our way."

"What's she like?" she asked, leaning into him.

"I don't know her," he replied, "but you've always said she was the most beautiful of the three and
the most flamboyant."

She looked up at him with a frown. "Didn't she
come to the wedding?"

"No, we eloped. You've told me she's complex,
though. Athena, too."

She groaned. "Tell me I'm not the simple, naive
one."

He laughed, squeezing her to him. "There's nothing simple about you, Gus. But you are a little naive.
Maybe because you have to relate to children so you
tend to trust with their openheartedness."

"You mean I'm gullible? A pushover?"

"Not at all. But it wouldn't hurt you to learn to be
a little more suspicious."

She went still against him. "I think that's happening," she said gravely. "It's one of the changes."

He knew that, but it still made him nervous to hear her say it. "You're suspicious of me," he said, trying to let her know he understood.

"Not you, necessarily," she said with a smiling glance at him. "But us. Does that upset you?"

"No," he said firmly. "Because we have a good relationship. Not quiet, necessarily, but good. As soon as you remember that, you'll get over the suspicions."

The sun went down with a bright, final spark.

They ate pasta with tomato and basil, and broccoli topped with melted cheese. She'd made shortbread cookies to have with their coffee.

He helped her clean up, then she went to bed early, complaining about her back. He was disappointed but not surprised when she chose her bed instead of his.

When he went to bed, he checked his bedside table and felt a moment's panic when he didn't see the phone. But he reached into the drawer and found that it had simply slipped a little farther back.

When he'd found her in his bedroom this morning, he'd felt fairly certain she was looking for the phone. He still wasn't convinced the laundry story was true, but it had flustered her and reminded him of some delicious moments in their past and therefore been worth it.

He felt for the Smith & Wesson under his pillow and settled down for the night.

He had to agree with her, he thought, as he found

himself listening for unfamiliar sounds, for anything out of the ordinary. He'd be glad when this was over.

He just wasn't anxious for her to regain her memory.

THE HUMMING SOUND OF AN INSECT woke him shortly after six in the morning. He sat up in bed, listening, wondering if he was losing his mind. He didn't see anything.

But there it was again, a little louder and not coming from inside the room at all, but outside. He leaped out of bed and went to the window, the very frail light of a cloudy dawn revealing a fly-sized speck on the horizon. It grew to the size of a bee in an instant, then before he could mutter a pithy expletive, the size of a robin.

It was a chopper. Mendez, he knew, had two restored Bell UH-1s.

He pulled on shoes and a shirt, looping the holster over his shoulder as he ran for Gusty's room. He flipped the light on, shouting her name.

"Gus! Gusty, wake up!" He went to her closet, grabbed a pair of leggings and the red sweater and tossed them at her while he looked for her shoes.

"What?" she asked, sitting up, rubbing her eyes. "Bram, what…?"

He found her shoes under the edge of the bed and knelt beside them to pull her legs over the side.

"Get dressed!" he ordered. "We're leaving."

"But…"

"Hurry up." He tried to convey urgency without

panic, though as he thought about running away through the mountains with a woman eight months pregnant, the panic was a little hard to control. "Get dressed, Gus!"

"Is it Mendez?" she whispered.

"I think so," he said, tying her right shoe. "I don't know how he found us. I took every pre—"

She was yanking on clothes, and he happened to glance at her just as her head surfaced from the neckhole of the sweater. Her eyes were wide with guilty shock, her arms frozen in the sleeves, the bunched-up sweater sitting atop her breasts now plump from the pregnancy.

They stared at each other a moment, she horrified, he silently scolding.

He yanked her sweater down and handed her the leggings. "Too late for that. Hurry." He had to help her stretch the leg opening over the shoes he'd already put on her, thinking that he'd been a cool and competent agent who almost never made a mistake. Why hadn't he trusted his gut and presumed she'd used the phone?

Because he was in love. He was about to become a father. His edge was compromised. The moment she had the slacks on he pulled her to her feet.

The sound of the helicopter's rotors had grown steadily until it was now a roar that sounded as though it was directly overhead.

Catching Gusty's hand, Bram ran her into the kitchen toward the back door. But through the kitchen window, he saw a second helicopter landing behind the house.

His options were narrowing. Escape was out. Standoff was all he had left. From the front of the house came the sound of glass breaking and the vicious thump of a door being broken down.

Gusty looked at him as though she fully expected him to have a solution.

He opened the mop closet and shoved her inside.

She pushed against the door as he tried to close it. "I am not going to hide in here while you—"

He closed the door on her protest, covered the few feet to the side of the kitchen in one stride and opened the window.

The mop closet door opened again and Gusty tried to get out, wielding a broom.

He took it from her and pushed her back in. "You stay there!" he snapped at her.

"Give me something!" she demanded. "A kitchen knife, anything. And I'll fight…"

He closed the door on her again an instant before Mendez walked into the kitchen, two tall, burly men flanking him. He was small in stature and wearing a designer suit. While working on the case, Bram had learned that Nicanor Mendez had been the brains of the family and Ramon, the ladies' man. Nicanor had always been protective of his younger brother and enjoyed the perks of Ramon's attraction to women. In repayment Nicanor provided him with the means to live in great style.

Each needed the other.

Bram guessed that Ramon Mendez's desperation and need for revenge stemmed more from his loss of income than from the absence of his sibling in his life. And that was why revenge had become murderous.

"Señor Bishop," Mendez said, stopping halfway into the kitchen. The two men behind him stood head and beefy shoulders above him. "I told you at the trial I would have my revenge. But when I learned you had a woman, I decided watching her die would hurt you more than the loss of your own life."

Bram reached deep down for the old steady nerves, the sharp assessment, the alternate plan.

But he didn't have them. Gusty stood behind him carrying their baby, nothing separating her from this madman but half an inch of plywood and Bram's own body.

He was resolved that that would have to do.

"It is unfortunate that your woman survived," Mendez said. "But I am here to take care of that. And then you. I've decided I will indulge myself and get rid of both of you."

Bram bluffed with a smile, "You're too late, amigo." He pointed to the drapes fluttering at the open window. "She's gone."

One of Mendez's bodyguards ran for the back door, but Mendez stopped him with a shout. "Idiot! I know this man. He would never send her off on her own. She is very pregnant." He made an exaggerated gesture of a rounded belly. "She is here. In the closet behind him, I think."

GUSTY, TERRIFIED BUT with a resolve born of no options, firmed her grip on the handle of a mop and waited for someone to yank the door open.

Instead, she heard the sharp crack of a gunshot. She gasped, but the sound went unheard as a high-pitched scream and various shouts and epithets boomed on the other side of the door.

"You *shot* me!" Mendez said in a tone of disbelief. "And you two! You didn't see a weapon?"

"Well, of course I shot you," Bram replied, his voice tinged with amusement. "Did you think I wouldn't?"

"But I have bodyguards!"

"Well, I think you have a legitimate suit against the employment agency that provided them."

"Are you going to do nothing?" Mendez's hysterical voice demanded, apparently of his bodyguards. "Take him! There are two of you!"

There was a moment of silence.

"Come on," Bram's voice taunted softly. "I can't get both of you at the same time, can I?"

"Well, what are you waiting for?!" Mendez demanded.

"I saw him," replied a strange, deep voice, "when they took Nicanor in. He tried to escape and this hombre shot a hole in his earlobe."

"I know that, but no man can do that twice!"

"We'll wait for Carlos and Luis."

There was more hysterical arguing, then the deep voice asked with sudden wariness, "Where *are* Carlos and Luis?"

"There!" Mendez said. "They are right..."

Another silence fell, then someone, probably the second bodyguard said, "The helicopter is empty. Why do they not come in?"

"Perhaps," Mendez said with high-pitched sarcasm, "they fear having their ears drilled like the two of you!"

Gusty listened to that last remark in disbelief, thinking that what had begun only moments ago as a terrifying incident was now taking on all the aspects of a comic opera.

But Bram's go-to-hell attitude frightened her. He was going to get himself killed if he didn't—

That thought was interrupted by a ripping pain across her abdomen. She put a hand to her mouth just in time to stifle a cry. She leaned against the side of the closet as another pain followed immediately.

Absently she heard something clatter to the opposite wall.

"She's in there, I tell you!" Mendez shouted. "Take him now!"

There was a gunshot and a shout, then a sudden commotion much louder than anything that had gone on before erupted beyond the closet door.

Was it rescue, Gusty wondered as an uncomfortable tightness replaced the pain in her stomach.

She heard new and different voices, commands to "Get him!" "Gun!" then Mendez's self-important voice. "I have been shot in the arm. You will please ask to have a plastic surgeon ready when I am taken to the hospital. I am sure this man has destroyed my biceps muscle!"

"You're just afraid," the deep-voiced bodyguard said, "that Maria will discover they're implants."

There was a shriek, then the sound of uproarious male laughter.

The door opened and Bram stood there, a fit-looking, middle-aged man in fatigues and a flack jacket at his side.

"Gus, this is Henry Wren," Bram said, "an old friend of mine. He's going to help us put Mendez and his boys away for a long time. Henry, the notorious Augusta."

"Notorious?" Gusty asked with a wince as the pressure seemed to tighten across her stomach.

"Because everyone's been looking for you." Bram caught her hand. "Are you okay?"

"Yeah. But you'd better help me out of here," she said, tightening her grip on him as the mounting pressure become another serious pain. "Or your son's going to be born in a mop bucket!"

THE DELIVERY ROOM in the Paintbrush hospital was mint-green and trimmed with a border paper of happy-looking pink cows jumping over smiling yellow moons. But right now, Bram couldn't focus on anything except for the lines of determination on Gusty's face.

He couldn't believe her. Courage was nothing new to him. He'd seen it in his friends repeatedly, and occasionally witnessed it in the reactions of an enemy. He'd tried to find it in himself.

But it was powerful stuff in the pale and perspiring face of a small-boned woman who'd wanted to fight at his side with a broom handle and was now determined, after five hours of what had seemed to him like a very grueling labor, to bring their child into the world.

He sat beside her and held her hand, and she'd long since ground his knuckles to powder. He couldn't remember ever loving anyone or anything this much—or praying this hard for a good outcome to anything.

"Okay, Gusty." Paunchy Dr. Grayson, a general practitioner in his late sixties, who looked like the quintessential country doctor, urged Bram to his feet. "We're going to get serious about pushing."

The nurse raised the head of the bed and pushed Bram to sit behind Gusty as the doctor drew her up into a sitting position.

Gusty fell back against him, her back hot and moist in the gown, her hair caught in a cap, a few soaking wet tendrils escaping.

She reached a hand behind her to touch his face. "I'm sorry about the phone." She'd said that a dozen times since they'd arrived at the hospital.

He'd told her a dozen times that it didn't matter.

"Gusty, forget the phone," he said, "and focus on the baby."

She sighed wearily. "I want to think about something else for a while," she teased, but the last word ended in a groan as another contraction came. They were relentless now, one after the other before she had time to recover.

"Push!" the doctor urged.

She did, a kind of primal growl escaping her as she gave it all she had.

"Okay, stop." The doctor, seated on a stool at the foot of the bed, smiled at her. "Good work. I see the top of a red head."

"Oh, no," Gusty groaned again. "Not red."

"Why not?" Bram asked.

"Because it had better be a girl. It's hard enough to be a redhead when you're a girl, but if you're a boy...ah!" Another contraction interrupted the thought then the doctor told her bracingly, "All right! We have the head. Let's go for a shoulder. Rest, Gusty, until the next contraction."

"Oh, yeah," she said. "Just what I need at this point in time. A four second res—ah!"

The shoulder was followed almost immediately by the second shoulder, then Bram's baby slipped into the world, wrinkled and screaming, little fingers already working.

A girl.

Bram's eyes scanned the tiny body anxiously as the doctor held her up. A pruney but perfect little face, limbs all there and well formed, nicely proportioned little body. Thank you, God! He felt himself relax for the first time in hours.

Gusty was shocked as they placed the baby in her arms.

"But I was so sure it was a boy!" she said, holding the blanket back to look into the little crimson face.

"A child's principal purpose in life," the doctor said, as he and the nurse smiled on the baby, "is to teach its parents that they don't know everything. We're going to have to take her back in a few minutes to weigh and measure her, so you and dad have a good look, but don't get too possessive."

"Bram, look!" Gusty said reverently, turning slightly so that she lay against his shoulder, giving him a good look at the baby. "I never would have guessed I was capable of making something this beautiful."

His arms wrapped around both of them, he put a fingertip to his daughter's cheek and marveled at the silky perfection of it. A dainty little mouth emitted very un-dainty screams, eyes shut tight against the cold, cruel world.

She was all protest and spirit and that touched something in him. There'd been a time when that *had been* him.

"It's all right," he told her quietly, slipping his hand under her head, wanting to feel her weight, wanting her to feel his strength. "We'll keep you safe. It's all right."

She stirred against him, and the screeches quieted to softer sounds of displeasure, of hunger.

Gusty looked at him, her eyes very close to his, and he saw something in them he'd wondered if he'd ever see again. It was a frail glimmer—but it was love.

He was encouraged by the knowledge that it wasn't remembered love but something brand-new—something inspired by all they'd shared in the short space of time she could recall.

She kissed him briefly, with a sincerity he felt to the marrow of his bones.

Then the doctor reclaimed the baby and the nurse shooed Bram out of the room. "Give us half an hour," she said. "There's a coffeepot in the waiting room, and a candy machine. I'll come and get you when we have her all tidied up."

All right, Bram thought, walking down the very short corridor to the waiting room. *This could all come right after all. I've been worried for nothing.*

Then he stepped out of the hall into the waiting room and realized it was far too early to congratulate himself.

Sitting on the room's blue vinyl sofa, leafing through magazines, were his best friends in the world—David Hartford and Trevyn McGinty.

"Hey!" he shouted happily, starting toward them.

Then advancing on him from two sides of the room where they'd apparently been pacing were two slender, redheaded women who, despite subtle differences in hair and style, could have been cloned from Gusty.

Athena and Alexis.

They did not look pleased with him.

Chapter Six

They converged in front of him and faced him shoulder to shoulder like some very small but very lethal attack force.

"Ladies." David appeared behind them. "This is Bram Bishop, our good friend, and the man who's kept Gusty safe all this time."

Bram suspected that last was added because the women were not convinced he was the good guy in all this.

"Bram, this is Athena Hartford, my wife."

Bram studied her in surprise. She had Gusty's beauty but none of the innocence in her eyes. She looked like a woman who couldn't be fooled. She was a lawyer, he remembered.

She wore jeans and a teal sweatshirt. Her hair fell long and straight and she looked every bit as though she could prevent it from curling at will.

The principal rule in any security mission was the conviction that you would prevail, conviction so strong that it was also clear to the enemy.

He smiled and reached out to shake her hand. "Hi, Athena," he said. "Gusty doesn't remember you, but she's been looking forward to the day you could all be together again." Then he remembered what else David had said. "You married this guy?" He asked skeptically, hooking a thumb in David's direction.

Her suspicion seemed to waver. "Ah, yes, I did. He's wonderful, and I guess I'll have to trust him when he tells me that you are, too."

"What's really wonderful," he corrected, "is your new niece. They're weighing her and doing some tests right now, but you can see her in a little while."

She seemed to melt. "Really? And they're both fine?"

"More than fine."

"Well, I see no reason why you couldn't have found some way to let us know that the two of you were all right!"

That scolding came from Alexis. Her hair waved riotously and was caught back loosely with some ruffly fabric thing. She wore black slacks and a black jacket, but a silky white collar of a blouse skimmed her firm chin. "We were beside ourselves with worry. All of us."

"Bram." Trevyn wandered up beside her and reached out to punch his arm. "Glad it's over. Meet *my* wife, Alexis McGinty."

"Your...?" Bram put a hand to his jaw in fresh amazement.

"Yeah. These Ames women have a fatal charm."

"Speaking of which..." Alexis caught Bram's

hand and ran her thumb over the wedding ring there. She looked at it wide-eyed. He barely held his stance when she yanked it closer so that her sister could see it.

"What does it mean?" Athena demanded.

He could do this. He smiled confidently. "That you were all blessed with the same charm. Gusty is *my* wife."

The five of them exchanged looks in silence.

"This is scary," Trevyn finally said. "We've faced death together and now we're all brothers-in-law?"

"So, it is your baby?" Alexis asked softly.

"Yes." He spoke with confidence in his new role.

Athena demanded, "And you love Gusty?"

"Of course."

She seemed relieved for a moment, then stomped her foot as her eyes sparked with fresh anger. "Then why did neither of you tell us you were married, or that she was pregnant?"

Before he could answer, she turned on David. "Did you know they were married?"

He shook his head.

"Did you?" she demanded of Trevyn.

"No," he replied. "But he was away on cases so much of the time, we barely saw him. And he never talks about himself."

"Well." Athena turned back to Bram. "What do you have to say for yourself?"

He made a quick decision. He felt like a rat doing this, but it sounded likely and, at the moment anyway, Gusty couldn't dispute it. "Gusty had her reasons.

I'm sure when she remembers, she'll want to tell you. But it isn't my place.''

Athena sputtered.

"Does that really matter right now?'' David asked. "You've prayed for her safety for almost a month, and now here she is, safe and sound. The baby's healthy and safe. Do you really need more than that?''

Athena sighed and turned to Alexis. "We do, don't we?'' she asked plaintively.

Bram had known they'd be very worried when he'd been forced to conceal Gusty, but he'd had no choice. Any contact would have risked discovery, as her phone call had ultimately proven.

Still he hadn't understood the depth of their misery in her absence until he saw it now in their eyes.

"We have to know,'' Alexis said finally, her manner relaxing, accepting. "But it can wait. As long as we know you love her.''

"He kept her safe,'' Trevyn reminded her. "You have your sister back, and you have your niece because of him.''

Alexis looked Bram over, her silent assessment apparently less than flattering, then she laughed lightly and flung her arms around him. "Oh, all right! Welcome to the family!''

Athena leaned in to hug him, as well, and he looked over their heads at his friends—and had a rude awakening.

They knew him as well as he knew himself, and they'd had the same commando training he'd had.

They didn't know *what* was wrong, although they knew something was.

David's dark eyes and Trevyn's watchful stance told him he was going to have to explain himself—and soon.

GUSTY COULD NOT BELIEVE how identical she and her sisters were. She had a thin memory of them as children, but they'd seemed different then.

Athena was smart, Alexis wild, and she, Gusty, had felt unprepared to follow either of them. She wondered why she could remember that little pocket of her past and nothing else.

She had absolutely no memory of the gorgeous women who leaned over her baby and cooed and fussed as though the baby was as precious an addition to their lives as she was to Gusty's.

And they'd married Bram's best friends. It seemed that love had blossomed while they'd all been allied in their search for *her*.

"Do you remember us at all?" Alexis asked.

If she could be glamorous instead of just naive, Gusty thought, she'd want to copy Lex's style. She shook her head. "Only a very brief memory of us as children. I remember being in a big house on the beach when we were supposed to have gone to Disneyland. We were all angry and grumbling about our parents and how little they cared about their promises to us."

"Ah, yes," Athena said. "We were nine and Dad

had promised us Disneyland because we'd all had brilliant report cards.''

''I can't imagine I was brilliant,'' Gusty challenged.

''You were,'' Athena assured her. ''You *are*. You understand the important things. Anyway, as a retired baseball player, Dad got a chance to be a featured celebrity on a cruise to Mexico, and Mom wanted to do that instead. So they went. We stayed with Aunt Sadie.''

Gusty put her fingertips to her forehead. ''Aunt Sadie,'' she repeated, then sighed. ''I saw her photograph at home, but don't remember her.''

''She looked a little like us,'' Alexis explained. ''She was Mom's sister and we spent a lot of time with her—summers, holidays. Her home, Cliffside, is the reason the three of us went to Oregon.''

Gusty was getting confused. ''I thought I went to meet you for your birthday,'' she said to Bram. ''And that it was in Washington.''

Now Athena looked confused.

Bram stepped in. ''She's talking about when the three of you crashed our costume party, Gus. Remember I told you that your aunt left David her home?''

She did, but she was a little overwhelmed with finally seeing her sisters, with all the new information. ''Yes, I think so.''

''Well, apparently your aunt had always promised the three of you the house, and you thought David might have somehow coerced her into leaving it to him. So you came to find out for yourselves what David and Trev and I were up to.''

She tried to make sense of the details. ''Did Sadie die?''

Athena bit her lip. Alexis nodded. ''In the crash of a little commuter plane while she was vacationing in Hawaii. Last March.''

Gusty wanted to feel grief, but she couldn't remember Sadie. That was the worst part of all this, she thought grimly. To have lost a loved one and not even remember her.

''She adored you,'' Athena said, tossing her hair back and playing with the baby's tiny hand. ''She used to call you an old soul, because you were wise about people and relationships and the ways of the world.''

She couldn't imagine that, but that information did solve another problem.

''We've been trying to think of a name for the baby,'' she said. ''I was so sure it was a boy, and we were going to name him Trevyn David.''

Both namesakes smiled.

''For a girl, we tried combining Athena and Alexis, but everything we came up with sounded strange. So maybe we should call her Sadie.'' She looked up at Bram. ''What do you think?''

He nodded instantly. ''I like it. Sadie Athena Alexis Bishop.'' He looked around at his friends and her sisters.

Everyone agreed it was perfect.

''We think you and Bram and Sadie should come

and live with us at Cliffside,'' Athena said. ''At least until you recover from all you've been through. It's bound to help Gusty regain her memory to be surrounded by family.''

''Athena and David and the boys live in the big house,'' Alexis explained. ''Trev and I have the guest house, and Bram used to live in the garage apartment, but you could switch with us. There'd be more room for the baby, and Trev and I have bought a house anyway. We're just waiting for it to be vacated at the end of the month.''

Gusty looked up at Bram, who was nodding. ''Living at Cliffside for a while is a good idea, but Trev, you've got all that photo equipment you have to have access to.''

Trevyn shook his head. ''I've opened my photo studio. Everything's moved there.''

''Or you could move into the big house,'' Athena suggested. ''There's lots of room.''

''The boys are noisy, though,'' David said. ''That might make it rough with a new baby.''

''What 'boys' are you talking about?'' Bram asked David.

''I've got custody of my little brothers now,'' David said. ''I keep forgetting that you haven't been around as much as Trevyn, even when we were in Chicago, and have never met them. They're living with us. They're no trouble, but they are a little rambunctious.''

''We'll be fine in the apartment.'' Bram smiled down at Gusty. ''Can you trust me on that?''

She'd trusted him with her life, she thought. And now she'd trust him with the baby's. There was no deeper commitment to another human being. Trusting him on a place to live seemed easy.

"Of course. But the doctor wants to keep the two of us a couple of days anyway. Sadie shows no sign of respiratory problems, but I guess that happens in premature babies, and he wants to make sure they don't develop."

It was odd to speak of her baby by name, to see that she was here and real and now part of a family plan. It made her feel changed.

Bram nodded. "That'll give me time to take care of a few things. I can call your school for you and tell them what's happened."

"Ask them to save my spot for next year," she said.

"Okay."

Alexis frowned with mock ferociousness. "You don't think we're going to let you move back to California now that we're all in Dancer's Beach, do you? Even if you did keep your marriage and your pregnancy to yourself."

Gusty blinked at that. "I did? Why?"

Athena shrugged. "That's the big question you have to answer for us when you start remembering things. And it better be good, because we're pretty upset with you."

Troubled by that, Gusty looked from one sister to the other. "Do I usually keep things to myself?"

"Not at all," Alexis replied. "You don't dwell on

bad news, but you love to share the good stuff.'' She glanced up at Bram. ''And though he hid you away from us for a long time, he looks like the good stuff to me. And the baby certainly does.''

''Then, maybe I should go back to California,'' Gusty teased, ''until I can come up with a good reason.''

''That might be wise,'' Trevyn said. ''Neither one of them is much for forgiving and forgetting. Or for minding her own business.''

''Now don't poison her against us until she remembers us,'' Athena said.

David laughed. ''At which point you can do it yourselves.''

Athena elbowed him in the stomach without even turning to look at him. ''You're going to love Dancer's Beach, and whether you remember us or not, after a couple of weeks there, you'll never want to live anywhere else. Trust me. I'm the one who knows everything.''

Alexis rolled her eyes. ''I maintain that if you have to tell everyone you know everything, it means you're not coming across that way. Am I right?''

Gusty smiled and used her only safety defense. ''I don't remember.''

The doctor shooed everyone out of the room, helped her nurse the baby, then removed Sadie to a bassinet beside Gusty's bed.

For most of a day, Gusty slept, nursed, slept, nursed, then spent the last hour, while the baby slept, weeping. Darkness had fallen and a driving rain beat against the roof and windows.

She remembered the last time she'd heard that sound—rain had been falling on the cabin roof as she lay wrapped in Bram's arms, cozy, warm and secure.

But that was over. They had to live in the real world and, while she'd anxiously awaited that eventuality when they'd been tucked away in the cabin, now faced with it, she wanted only to turn back the clock.

"Augusta!" Bram's gentle voice whispered in concern as he leaned over the side of her bed and turned her face toward him. The room was in darkness, except for the small light on the wall behind her. "What's wrong?"

She gave him a belligerent side-glance and focused on her feet, a sight she hadn't seen in the past month and a half.

"What *isn't* wrong?" she asked testily. "How am I going to raise a baby when I can't remember anything?"

"You have life knowledge," he reminded her. "That's all you need for a while. And you'll have help—me, your sisters, their husbands."

"Where are they, by the way?" she asked.

"I took everybody to the cabin and came back to spend the night with you."

He'd hoped that would earn him a smile, but all he got was a wondering look that morphed almost instantly into a quarrelsome grimness. "Did you see how beautiful and confident they are?" She folded her arms petulantly over the blanket. "How connected they seem to each other? I don't remember that. I wonder if I ever had it. Did I belong as their sister, or was I the one who never fit in? The one who was always afraid to follow?"

He rubbed a knuckle along her cheekbone. "Your aunt called you the old soul, remember. The one who understood relationships. You must have belonged."

She looked at him hopefully. "Do you think I did?"

He wanted to, but he couldn't lie about that. "Today was the first time I've seen the three of you together. But I know *you*. You give everyone everything you have in the way of love and trust and support. I'm sure you belonged. You're just suffering what's probably a very normal letdown after such a major assault on your body and your emotions. Not to mention what went on this morning and for the past three weeks."

"I wonder why I didn't tell them I got married?" she asked moodily.

He tucked a wayward strand of hair behind her ear and shook his head.

"Or that I was pregnant?"

That he could answer honestly. "I don't know. I'm sure you had your reasons."

"But what could they be? Unless I thought I didn't belong."

"I think you'll just have to answer that when you get your memory back."

She sighed and idly kicked a foot under the covers.

"I thought having the baby might bring it back. You know—stress and all that."

"No, I'd say you were forced to be too focused on having the baby for any part of your brain to explore anything else."

She patted his hand on the rail of her bed. "You do have all the answers."

"Then why," he asked with a smile, "are you worried?"

She sighed wearily and closed her eyes. "I wish you could climb in here with me," she said so quietly he had to lean down to hear. "I've never slept as well as I did that night."

She fell asleep before she could finish the sentence. But he didn't have to hear the end of it. He remembered that night, too. He'd had her warm, soft bottom curled against his groin, torturing him, the mound of her belly and their gently moving baby under one arm, the full curve of her breast in his other hand. He hadn't slept a wink.

And he probably wouldn't, either, for a long time to come.

An infant who didn't know night from day would be a demanding taskmaster.

And so would a guilty conscience.

But exhaustion and loss of peace of mind were a small price to pay for what he wanted.

THEY WENT BACK to the cabin two days later. Athena and Alexis had packed her things and Bram's and they'd all piled into Paintbrush's only cab and ridden to the small local airport. There they were met by a small plane David had hired for the trip home.

"I never thought to ask how you got to Paintbrush," Bram asked as he helped Trevyn load bags.

"Wren sent a chopper for us. Pays to have connections. David hired him to look for Gusty right after she disappeared." He paused to grin at him and correct himself. "Right after you took her from the hospital. He's had Athena's office and home phone bugged and picked up Gusty's call about the same time Mendez did."

The bags loaded, Bram closed the door, then climbed into the back of the plane with Gusty and the baby.

As her sisters and his friends took their seats, he leaned forward. "I understand that Athena and Alexis probably saw Gusty's photo on television and went to Oregon to find her, but how did you guys get involved?"

"The night of the party," David said, "I'd spent time with Athena, but we hadn't exchanged names, I'd just glimpsed her face for an instant before I passed out."

"Passed out?"

David dismissed that detail with a shake of his head. "That's a long story. The point is I saw Gusty's photo on TV, thought she was the woman I'd been with that night and ran to the hospital to her rescue, only to find her gone—thanks to you. I thought she was carrying my baby and was determined to find her."

"You mean, you two...?"

"That's a long story, too."

Trevyn turned in his seat. "It was the same thing with me. I'd been with Alexis, and apparently not giving us their names was part of the plot to find out what we were up to with the house. I was in Canada doing a calendar shoot and when I came out of the woods to civilization and watched television my first night across the border, I thought Gusty was Alexis and that she was carrying *my* baby."

"You and Alexis...?"

"No. Also long and complicated. But you two apparently did?"

That was easily answered—and, as a nice bonus— it was the truth.

"No, we didn't. But she did tell me she taught school in Pansy Junction before she ran off like Athena and Lex. So I tracked her down and spent four days with her, winning her over."

"But you came back to Cliffside and never said a word."

"I worked from here, but for reasons Gusty will reveal when she remembers them, she didn't want anyone to know. So I kept it to myself."

"We eloped," Gusty contributed.

"Men," Athena said with an aggrieved air.

"Yeah," Alexis added with a grim glance at him.

"I can't imagine what those reasons were," Gusty said, her voice quiet and sad. "I'm so sorry I did that to you."

"Don't worry about it," Alexis instructed with a

smile over her shoulder. "You have good reasons for everything you do. And one day you'll remember. Until then, we're going to live happily ever after in Dancer's Beach, the Ames sisters, the Three Musketeers, and their brilliant and beautiful offspring."

"Hear, hear!" they all shouted.

Happily ever after, Bram repeated to himself as the pilot started the motor. God, he hoped so.

GUSTY FOUND CLIFFSIDE completely unfamiliar, but a beautiful place. There was a large two-story brick home that appeared Colonial in style. The trim and shutters were white, and shrubs and bushes crowded beneath the first-floor windows. What looked like a guest house in the same design, though smaller, sat between it and a four-car garage, above which was an apartment.

A broad lawn stretched thirty yards or so toward bushes at the edge of a cliff that rose above the ocean. Athena pointed to the big house. "It might help you remember things to walk through it, but I'm sure you must be tired and want to save that for later. Dotty, David's housekeeper, has cleaned up your apartment and left some meals in the freezer."

"She also laid in diapers, wipes, formula, that sort of thing." Alexis gave the baby in Gusty's arms a loving pat. "But if you need anything else, any of us would be happy to run out for you."

As though on cue, a woman peered out the front door, went back inside, then reappeared instantly with two young boys in tow and a deliriously happy black dog the size of a small pony striking out ahead.

With a broad smile, David left the group and started toward them. The dog leaped on him, happily accepting a ruffling of his floppy ears, then moved on toward where everyone else waited.

The boys broke into a run and ran into David's embrace hugging him heartily, then stepped back and slugged his arms and shoulders with manlike affection.

Gusty guessed they were preteen, the slender fair-haired boy probably several years older than the shorter stocky one.

Trevyn, Alexis and Athena greeted the dog.

"Gusty, Bram, Sadie," Athena said, "this is Ferdie, Brandon and Brady's dog."

He had a black-and-white face and a giant tongue that slurped every hand and face he could reach.

"I know he looks as though he's been assembled of mixed breed parts, but we think he's Great Dane and Saint Bernard. He just adopted the boys one day in the park, and they brought him with them when they moved in with David."

Gusty scratched his ears while Bram stroked the long, lean back. Ferdie whined in ecstasy.

The boys dealt with, David reached down to hug the woman with them. She wore an apron and an air of efficiency.

"Gus, this is Dotty," Bram said, drawing her closer. "Our housekeeper, and general do-gooder for all of us. She's also an excellent cook, so the two of you will have to match skills some time.''

Dotty oohed over the baby and won Gusty's heart. ''Isn't she the prettiest little thing? And another redhead. Does this mean life's going to get even livelier around here?''

David groaned theatrically. ''Saints preserve us!''

''Were you kidnapped?'' the dark-haired boy asked Gusty. He had alert brown eyes and a sweet smile as he looked into Sadie's face. ''Did they have a gun? Were you scared?'' Then he noticed Bram and pointed to him, eyes wide. ''*You're* the scary-looking guy!''

David brought the boys to Bram. ''Yeah, he is pretty ugly, but he's also my good friend. So there was nothing to worry about after all. Bram, Gusty—'' David touched the dark head of the boy admiring the baby ''—this is Brady.'' Then he turned to the fair-haired older boy. ''And Brandon.''

To Bram he explained, ''The boys saw the two of you at the airport when they flew here to live with me. When they arrived, Athena was at the house and they recognized her, thinking it was her they'd seen. They told us she was with a 'scary-looking guy.'''

Hands on his hips, Bram pretended to frown down at the boys. ''So you guys are afraid of me?''

Brandon shook his head. ''Not now that we know you're a good guy. You play basketball?''

''Better than David.''

Brady laughed. ''Anybody's better than David.''

David heaved a long-suffering sigh and smiled

thinly at Bram. "You might as well know now. That's what you're up against when you raise children. Ingratitude and harassment. Lots of harassment."

"So, you guys got married, too," Brandon exclaimed. "Jeez, everybody's getting married around here."

Dotty put an arm around each of the boys. "That's because there's lots of love at Cliffside. Come on, boys, let's get out of the way. I'm sure everybody's tired after their trip and anxious to relax."

Brandon snapped his fingers and the dog ran to him. He called to Bram over his shoulder. "One-on-one tomorrow afternoon?"

"You got it!" Bram shouted back. Then he asked David, "How'd you get two cute, smart kids like that for brothers anyway?"

David grinned. "Different fathers. You two go home. We'll get out of your hair. Just know how glad we are that you're safe and sound."

Gusty hugged each of her sisters, then their husbands, touched by their generosity. She must have belonged, she told herself, if they cared this much.

Bram hugged Alexis, then Athena, then shook hands with his friends. "I owe you big, guys. Thanks."

Athena blew them a kiss. "We won't bother you, so call us when you need something, or if you just want to be in touch."

"But if it's going to be days," Alexis cautioned, "I warn you, one of us will be coming for the baby.

Incidentally, we asked around and got the name of a good pediatrician, and an OB-GYN, too.''

''Thanks, you two.''

As the group walked away toward the big house, bags in hand, talking about opening a bottle of champagne and celebrating their safe return, Bram led Gusty up the stairs at the side of the garage and into the apartment above.

It had very masculine furnishings, a distressed leather sofa and a large matching chair, a green-and-gold-plaid stadium blanket tossed over the back to soften it. The coffee table was a campaign trunk, the end tables brass containers of some kind that were tall and narrow.

''Those are interesting,'' Gusty said, pointing to one of them with her free hand. ''What do they hold?''

''Ammunition,'' he replied, carrying her bags into the apartment's only bedroom. ''Only, not anymore.''

The apartment was small in terms of number of rooms, but the kitchen and living room were a generous size, and separated by a long kitchen counter at which four stools were lined up.

It was apparent that Dotty had dusted, scrubbed and vacuumed. The scent of a pine cleaner lingered in the air.

''I found those boxes at that antiques shop in town when we first came here,'' he shouted out to her. ''They don't offend you, do they?''

''Not at all.''

She stood in the bedroom doorway, watching him

push his clothes to one side of the closet, presumably to make room for hers.

"We don't have to share the room," he said, turning to smile at her. "I can sleep on the sofa. But we will have to share the closet. The apartment's a little short on storage space. Looks like Dotty added a few extra hangers when she tidied up."

He came to take the baby from her. "I'll hold her while you put your things away. I'm best with her when she's sleeping."

They'd been up together with her most of the night before and she'd noticed that morning that he was already handling her with less nervousness than he had the first day.

He sat on the edge of the bed with her and pulled off the little woolen hat that went with the outfit Athena and Alexis had bought Sadie at the Mathews Mercantile.

"We're going to need some baby furniture," he said absently, seemingly completely absorbed in studying Sadie's face.

Gusty decided it was time to broach a subject she'd been thinking about since the day Sadie was born. She went to the suitcase and carried her few articles of clothing to the closet. She ignored the thought of how poorly they would fit now that she was no longer pregnant.

"I've been thinking about that," she said, hanging up the big, baggy dress, her back to Bram.

"Baby furniture?" he asked, then added, his voice laced with amusement, "or ammunition?"

She stepped a little deeper into the closet—a defense mechanism, she guessed.

"About sharing the room," she said, without turning around. "We should. Babies are very sensitive to their surroundings, and I can't have her thinking I've alienated her father just because I don't remember our past together. I think we *should* share the room."

She hung up the hooded sweatshirts and folded the leggings over the base of a hanger.

When he still hadn't commented, she turned to face him, afraid he thought it a bad idea, and found him standing right behind her. He'd put the baby down in the middle of the bed.

He'd effectively blocked her in the closet doorway and there was no way around him.

Not that she wanted one.

In jeans and a gray sweatshirt emblazoned with the Mathews Mercantile's logo, he represented everything that had made her feel safe at the cabin, and now everything that would protect her in her real life.

He pinched her chin between his thumb and forefinger and tipped her face up. His eyes were watchful, gentle. "You're sure?"

"Yes," she replied with conviction, then wondered for the first time if she might be asking too much of him. "But will that be hard for you? I mean, our sharing a bed when I can't make love for a good six weeks."

It occurred to her that that was presuming a lot, and she tried to backpedal. "Not that you'd necessarily *want* to, but if you did..." He wasn't saying anything, just watching her with a small smile, and she didn't seem to be able to stop talking.

"I mean, I'm not suggesting that I consider myself *that* desirable that you wouldn't be able to stand it, but if you *did* want…"

He raised his hand from her chin to cover her mouth. "Yes, it will be hard. Yes, I want to. Yes, you are desirable. But I'll find a way to stand it because I have missed holding you. Though I'm not sure it's a good idea to do this just for the baby."

"But I want her to feel secure."

He nodded. "So do I. But I want *you* to feel secure, too. You're as important to me as she is."

God. How could she not remember this man? Without inhibition, she let herself fall against him and wrapped her arms around his waist.

"I'm sorry for all this has put you through," she said against the front of his shirt, imagining what it must be like to love someone the way she was beginning to love him and have them not remember your touch, your whispers, your claim to their secrets.

His arms closed around her and he pressed her to him. "Nothing was your fault. And not remembering isn't your fault. It'll come back. Just be patient." Then he tipped her face up and kissed her, making any attempt at patience impossible.

It began sweetly, a tender exploration on his part to gauge her reaction.

But she'd been trying to hide a need for him, to suppress all the strong feelings she held and had been just a little ashamed of, because she had no memory of him and therefore no apparent basis for them. But that didn't matter anymore. She was making the commitment to be his, to make him hers, to make a family for their baby.

She opened her mouth to him, and after one surprised moment, he responded, taking the kiss from tenderness to passion. His hands roamed her back and hips as his tongue explored her mouth. Her fingertips gripped his shoulders as she stood on tiptoe to kiss him back with all the excitement of feelings finally unguarded.

He drew away at last, gasping for air, putting a hand to the closet doorway to steady both of them.

"Okay, wait," he said breathlessly. "We're forgetting the six-week rule here. One more minute of this…"

She dropped her forehead to his shoulder. "I know, I'm sorry. I…it's like it's new to me."

He patted her shoulder, drawing a steadying breath. "Don't apologize. But I thought women who'd just delivered babies were supposed to have low libidos."

She laughed lightly against him. "Well, see, I don't remember that. And that's the kind of life knowledge you don't have if it's your first baby." She looked up at him in mock alarm. "It *is* my first baby? I didn't have one with the activist, the stockbroker or the prince?"

"No." He kissed her quickly, soundly. "You didn't feel that deeply about anyone until me."

"I guess I have some smarts after all."

Chapter Seven

"What kind of pasta?" Shrugging into his jacket, Bram examined the grocery list Gusty had given him. "Angle what?"

She grinned at him from the sofa where she nursed Sadie. "Not angle. *Angel*-hair. That really thin noodle. I like it best in tomato sauce, don't you?"

He leaned over her and kissed her forehead. He loved the sight of her nursing Sadie, the small, veined marble swell of her breast above the greedily rooting little face, both mother and baby apparently happy with their work.

"Actually, we have the pasta argument all the time. You like the small stuff, I like the shells."

"Then get the shells," she said. "And don't forget the infant seat and the crib. The crib doesn't have to be anything fancy, just make sure it's up to safety standards as far as the width between the upright rungs."

He raised an eyebrow at that. "Did you remember

that that's been in the news? Or is that just life knowledge considering you're now a mother?''

She frowned. "I don't know. Doesn't matter, I guess."

He liked hearing her say that. Her anxiousness over her memory seemed to have diminished somewhat with the arrival of the baby, and she was more relaxed.

"Do we have money to buy a crib?" she asked suddenly. "I've been thinking about that. Without me teaching or you working for a month, what are we living on?"

"We have a healthy savings account," he assured her, his hand on the front door. "You had an inheritance."

"What's your money from?" she insisted.

"I worked all those years with no family, no expenses, and a tendency to save my money," he replied. "When I worked for the CIA, my off-time cover was as a personal guide in dangerous parts of the world. I made a bundle. So we're comfortable."

Her eyes were now wide. "How comfortable?"

"Middle six-figures comfortable."

She gasped. "You're kidding!"

"I'm not. Sadie can go to college without a scholarship. Though I'm sure she'll be smart enough to earn one."

"Do you miss that life?" she asked. "I mean is father and husband going to seem horribly dull after…"

He had to laugh at that. "Has it seemed dull to you so far?"

She laughed, too. "I don't know what's gone before, but the last month has been most eventful."

"There you have it. Okay, I'm—" He was interrupted by a firm knock on the door. He pulled it open and stood looking into the lit tip of a cigar in the jaw of a portly middle-aged man in coveralls.

"Bishop?" the man asked.

"Yes."

"Furniture's here."

"But I didn't—"

Bram's protest was cut off by a very loud "This is it, Jimbo!" and the surprisingly agile and graceful disappearance of the coveralled man down the stairs. Another man opened the back of a truck. Emblazoned on the side was Baby, Baby! with a bespectacled and very sophisticated looking stork leaning on the exclamation point.

"What is it?" Gusty asked, putting Sadie to her shoulder and rebuttoning her blouse.

"I think it's baby furniture," he replied. "You know anything about that?"

"No." Patting the baby's back, she went to the side window and looked down onto the driveway.

As he watched from the doorway, Coveralls carried up a collapsed crib made of golden oak with a plump duckling decal on the side, and Jimbo followed with a mattress and other accessories.

Athena and Alexis came from the direction of the big house. They disappeared around the back of the truck, then reappeared, one carrying an infant seat, the other a lamp with a Minnie Mouse base.

"What—?" Bram began as Athena topped the stairs.

"We didn't get to throw Gusty a shower," she interrupted, walking past him toward the bedroom, "so the least we could all do is see that Sadie has what she needs."

"*My* job is to see that Sadie has…"

"Look." Athena stood toe to toe with him, the infant seat held in one hand. "Your job is to be what you say you are and to make my sister happy. As her sister, *my* job is to do everything I can to help her do *her* job."

"Yeah." Alexis stepped up, holding the lamp aloft, looking a little like some Disney-created Lady Liberty. "The guys have told us how tough you are, how possessive and protective. But don't think you're going to muscle us out, because you aren't. She belongs to you, but she belongs to us, too, and we haven't seen her in about eight months, thanks to you, so…so watch yourself."

Okay. They'd welcomed him into the family, but apparently all was not forgiven. He could remember a few times of desperate peril in his career when he could have used their intimidation techniques.

"Now that was a little strong," Gusty said, coming up beside him, the baby on her shoulder. "All he did was take care of me. I'm sorry you were worried, but it isn't fair to take it out on him. You owe him an apology."

Athena and Alexis looked at each other, then at Gusty.

"You're not usually one to tell others what to do," Athena said.

"Yeah," Alexis added. "Particularly us."

Gusty smiled. "I don't remember how I was. But this is how I am now. Don't abuse my husband, or you'll answer to me. Adorable baby furniture or not." Athena and Alexis shared another look that turned into reluctant smiles.

"I apologize," Athena said.

"And I'm sorry, too." Alexis handed him the lamp. "We just didn't want you to think we're giving her up completely, however much you love her."

"I wouldn't think of asking you to do that."

"Good. Then we understand one another." Alexis went back down the stairs and Athena carried the car seat into the living room.

Bram couldn't remember the last time he'd been defended by a woman.

She reached up to plant a kiss on his cheek. "Get the pasta shells," she said, taking the lamp from him.

His head was spinning and his heart was flipping. Not a condition conducive to negotiating stairs.

He didn't have to worry about that, though, because he suddenly found himself flanked by David and Trevyn.

"We were just coming up to get you," David said, turning to lead the way down the stairs.

"I'm going to the market," he said, slapping his

shirt pocket. "I'm very domestic now. Gusty gave me a list."

"That's just what we want to talk to you about." Trevyn followed along behind.

"But I can't talk now," he said. "It's after five and the market'll close if I—"

"We'll drive you." David caught his arm and re-directed him from the Jeep to his blue sedan.

Bram stopped in his tracks. "You're coming grocery shopping with me?" he asked in disbelief.

"It's do that while the girls are occupied," Trevyn said, opening the right rear door of the car, "or discuss all the inconsistencies in your story in front of them."

Great. He'd thought when he'd left the government service he was finished with interrogation. He climbed into the back of the car. David backed out of the garage, with Trevyn riding shotgun, and drove down the driveway to the road that led to town.

He stopped at the bottom of the hill, then headed for Coast Groceries on the edge of downtown Dancer's Beach.

Bram struggled to organize his thoughts. In the first place, he wasn't accustomed to having to explain himself and that presented its own difficulties. But these were his friends and he understood their concerns. They were both married to Gusty's sisters, and their relationships had been established in their search for her.

Now that she'd been found in his care, with his

baby, and because he was their friend, he would be required to answer their questions.

"In your own words would be fine," David said, locating him in the rearview mirror.

"And in this lifetime," Trevyn added, looking at him over his shoulder, "would be preferable."

He was not going to get out of this.

"We met at the costume party," he began reluctantly, "just like you did. Only I, obviously being the superior agent of the three of us, was able to find her again in a matter of days. I went to see her to get to know her, to see if this…this burning in my gut was something permanent."

He could feel it now. It had started when she'd run away from him that night and continued until he'd tracked her to Pansy Junction and she'd opened her front door.

He could see David's frown in the mirror, as though he related.

"Yeah," Trevyn said, as though he did, too. "Go on."

"For four days we walked the hills around her place, made love, talked about sharing our future, then she had to go back to school and I was just getting the agency started. I went home and the plan was that we'd keep in touch by phone, and get married Easter weekend."

"'The plan *was*,'" Trevyn repeated. "You say that as though it didn't happen."

Bram drew a breath, then let it out slowly. "It didn't."

David caught his eye again in the mirror. "Then you're *not* married?"

He had to say it. "No."

"But she thinks you are," Trevyn pointed out.

"I told her we were," he said. Then he added grimly, "She doesn't remember that we never did it."

"But your rings…"

"I bought them in Astoria. Well, Warrenton, actually. I put mine on when I went to get her out of the hospital, and put hers on her before I woke her up. I told her I was her husband, showed her my third finger and hers, and she believed me." That still surprised him a little, but he hadn't given it any more thought. "Since she didn't remember anything, I didn't think she'd come with me unless I could convince her it was safe."

David shook his head. "Wren said you were hiding her from the brother of a client you put away in August."

"Right."

"How did he know about her if you guys never got married? Were you still seeing each other?"

"No. She called to tell me she'd changed her mind, that it was over and I didn't hear from her again until she called and said she wanted to meet me somewhere private to talk.

"I suggested the Shelldrake. I registered under an old alias because my name had been in the press a lot because of the Mendez conviction, and if she wanted privacy to reconcile, I was going to insure it. But apparently Mendez followed me, intending to kill me, then saw me with Gus. My guess is that when we left the inn separately, he thought she'd be easy pickings by herself and that would hurt me more than killing me. He rammed her car into the water and you know the rest of it. The pilot boat picked her up.''

''Where were you at that point?''

''Not far behind her. We'd fought all weekend, but the quarrel before we left was a beaut. She took off. I had to settle up with the desk, then followed her, determined to catch her and make her listen to reason. I was probably eight or ten car lengths behind her when she went into the river.

''I jumped in after her, but I saw the pilot boat get her so I went back to my car. Mendez saw me and followed me. I lost them in the back roads of Astoria. Then the news on my car radio was talking about the girl they'd fished out of the river. She had a head injury, no ID and didn't know who she was. I knew I had to get to her before Mendez did.''

''Why didn't you call the police?'' Trevyn asked.

''Because I knew I could keep her safer than they would. I'd just dealt with the Mendez family. They were ruthless and vengeful. I just wish I'd been more on my guard earlier, but Gusty had my entire focus.''

''So, all wet from the river, you walked into a department store to buy rings then stole her away from the hospital?''

He gave the back of Trevyn's shoulder a shove. ''I had luggage that *didn't* end up at the bottom of the river. I sat in the dark for a few minutes, trying to concoct a plan. I figured I could get her to come with me if I could convince her I was safe—if I told her I was her husband. Rings would make that more convincing. I've done a case or two in Astoria. The Warrenton Fred Meyer store has everything, including jewelry. I bought a simple set, drove back to the hospital, parked in the trees. For a while there were lots of police, lots of press, then things finally quieted down. I got her from the hospital just before dawn.''

"You took her to Pansy Junction."

"I did, thinking it'd help her relax. She was agitated and upset, and I thought even if she didn't remember anything, familiar things might somehow help her."

"I've got a question," Dave said, pulling into the grocery store's parking lot. "When she finally phoned you and asked you to meet her after all that long period of no contact, she must have told you why she'd refused to marry you."

Bram sighed. This had all been exhausting the first time through. Living it again was no easier. "She had an amniocentesis test as part of her prenatal care and it suggested something was wrong with the baby."

David parked near the door and turned off the motor, then turned in his seat to face him.

Trevyn spun around. "What?"

"Yeah. They expected the baby to have major problems," he repeated. "She thought I wouldn't be able to deal with it. Anyway, five months later when she had an ultrasound, they told her everything was fine—the baby had no apparent problems. That was when she called me."

Trevyn frowned. "Then why did you fight all that weekend? Didn't she want to reconcile?"

"I wanted to get married right away. She wanted to wait. She wanted to be certain the baby was perfect, and she just wanted me to bow out until it was born."

"Man."

"Yeah. I told her what I thought of that in no uncertain terms, that she wasn't just walking away with my baby. War was waged. By the time she stormed away, she told me she hated me and she never wanted to see me again." He sighed, realizing now as he heard himself retell the story, the staggering magnitude of what he'd done. "Then Mendez pushed her into the water and she forgot everything. Opportunist that I am, I took advantage of her amnesia."

"It was a way to get her away and keep her safe," Trevyn said. "I've resorted to a desperate measure or two with Lex myself. And there was no baby involved."

David nodded. "After all we've done in the name of justice," he said, "it's hard to fault you for that one. But you're going to pay big time, buddy, when she starts remembering."

"Tell me about it."

"And living so close to the Terrible Twosome," Trevyn said. He added by way of explanation, "That's Athena and Alexis."

Bram made a scornful sound. "Did you really think you had to explain that?"

"She's going to remember soon," Trevyn finished. "You better be ready with some smooth talking."

"How many times have you seen me lose?" he asked, unbuckling his seat belt.

"You have an unblemished record," David said. "But we're not talking just seasoned international terrorists, here."

"Yeah," Trevyn added. "We're talking *women*. Angry women. Righteously indignant women." He added pityingly, "You have no idea what you're up against."

ATHENA SAT in the newly delivered Boston rocker, singing to Sadie in a slightly off-key soprano. They'd had to put the rocker in the living room because the good-sized bedroom was cluttered almost to impassability with an entire set of matching baby furniture.

"We knew it'd be too much for this place," Alexis said as she made tea in the kitchen. "But we figured you should be equipped for when we moved out of the guest house and you move in. Then you'll have everything you need."

"But it's too generous!" Gusty protested. She lay stretched out on the sofa per Athena's orders, resting. "Bram tells me we're very stable financially, and I..."

"Doesn't matter," Alexis said. "We've always taken care of you."

Gusty propped up on an elbow. "Why is that?" she asked as Lex put a cup of tea on the trunk beside her. "Tell me the truth now. Am I the cowardly one?

Why do I have that impression? Because I don't re-member anything except that childhood image I told you about. But I sort of *feel* as though you're both very brave and I'm not.''

Athena closed her eyes and shook her head. Sadie slept peacefully.

''That's Mom's influence. She didn't like us very much and bolstered her own ego by hammering us. She liked me a little because I could be as mean as she was, but she was always telling Lex she was a useless dreamer, and you that you were afraid of your own shadow. But you weren't. You just weren't ad-venturous. You always loved the simple things that were right around you.''

Lex sat at Gusty's feet and patted the toes of her white socks. ''You were always very domestic. We knew you'd be a great mother.''

''What about our father?'' Gusty asked, sitting up to sip at her tea.

''Nice guy,'' Athena replied, ''but more into peace than justice. He did whatever kept Mom placated.''

''So the cruise instead of Disneyland.''

''Right.'' Alexis stirred sugar into her tea. ''We all grew up with hang-ups. Athena has moments of hat-ing herself because she's afraid the clever lawyer in her is something she got from our manipulative mother. And I completely lost my ability to paint for a while because I'd tried so hard to not be like Mom at all that I hardly knew who I was. So I couldn't produce anything worthwhile.''

Athena smiled. "Until she did a very revealing portrait of Trevyn."

Gusty waited for one of them to explain, but they simply moved on.

"And when you remember who you are," Athena said, "you'll remember that you're the sane one who always knows us best. When I don't know what to do about Lex, you tell me what she's feeling and why I'm reacting to it the way I do. When Lex is mad at me, you make her give me some slack."

Gusty winced. "Then everyone must hate me. I sound like the know-it-all child in class."

Lex put an arm around her. "Absolutely not. You're always very sweet and charming about it." She paused and amended, "Well, usually. If we don't listen, you tend to get testy."

"The last couple of days at the cabin," Gusty said, leaning into Lex, astonished by how close she felt to her sisters already, even without much memory of them, "Bram told me about the two of you and I was afraid you probably hated me because you hadn't come to my wedding. Then he told me I didn't even tell you about it. I wonder why I did such a thing." Gusty sat up and frowned at one sister, then the other. "Particularly if I was the one who wanted all of us to get along. Why would I have hurt you like that?"

"Right now it doesn't matter," Athena said. "Right now we have to think about dinner for you two." She glanced at the clock. "Dotty left all kinds of things in the freezer. Want me to defrost something?"

"Defrosting is what we do best," Alexis said. "When she was single, Athena lived on deli food, and I'm into creative uncooked stuff. Salad in a tortilla, chick peas in a pita pocket. Trevyn thinks it's awful, so he cooks. Clever, aren't I?"

Gusty nodded. "I asked Bram to bring home pasta. I saw tomato sauce in the cupboard and there's salad makings, so that'll be easy. I wonder what's taking them so long."

Alexis sighed theatrically. "Oh, they probably found some injustice they had to put right and they're skulking through the produce aisle right now, ridding the world of eggplant."

Gusty exchanged a grin with Athena. "That would never have occurred to me."

"That's because you're not the nutty one," Athena said.

WHEN BRAM ARRIVED HOME, Alexis stood at the top of the garage apartment stairs, wearing an apron, Ferdie standing beside her. The dog raced down the stairs, then ran around crazily, barking as they unloaded the groceries.

"Why are you in costume, sweetheart?" Trevyn asked Alexis, pulling a bag of potatoes out of the trunk.

"Ha-ha!" she replied. "No brownies for you. I was going to tell you and David not to go home. We're having dinner here."

Trevyn focused on the important piece of information. "We have brownies?"

"Frosted and everything," she said haughtily. "Gus and Dotty are making them. But I'm eating yours. Hurry on up. We need the pasta."

David handed Bram a grocery bag. "Brace yourselves, men. It's like the missing piece of a juggernaut has been found and it's going to roll over all of us."

Bram had trouble finding fault with the juggernaut.

First of all, it was gorgeous. The three Ames sisters, missing piece installed, were scurrying around the apartment, their perfumes blending magically with the delicious aromas from the kitchen to make the place smell like every man's dream come true: women *and food.*

Gusty, apparently the only one of the three with any real skill in the kitchen, was clearly in command. She issued softly spoken orders and manned the spoon in a very large pan of tomato sauce. Dotty kept an eye on something in the oven while Gusty sent Brandon and Brady out to the table with salad dressings, Parmesan cheese, glasses, a pitcher of milk, a carafe of coffee.

The table had been moved into the living room for space and another table comandeered from somewhere had been added on the end. The whole had been covered with what appeared to be a king-size bedsheet. A pot of some pretty weed had been placed in the middle.

David uncorked a bottle of wine while Trevyn counted chairs. Bram got to sit in the rocker with Sadie.

He didn't bother to wonder why the woman who'd

given birth four short days ago was on her feet in the kitchen. He imagined her sisters had tried to discourage her, but she was the kind of woman people naturally gathered around for physical and emotional sustenance. She liked to do for others and being deprived of what she considered a privilege would have been worse for her than being tired or having pain.

He was relieved to see how well the sisters got along. He hadn't known much at all about their relationship, and after listening to Gusty worry over it in the cabin, he'd been afraid there might be a problem there.

Clearly, there wasn't. They teased and harassed each other, but they cared and, though she might have hurt them in ways none of them understood right now, they loved her anyway. He was relieved for her.

They ate, crowded around the table, Sadie asleep in Bram's arm, oblivious to the big noisy family she'd been born into. Ferdie lay stretched out under the table between their feet.

Bram was grateful for it himself. In the bleak eternity of his childhood, he'd wondered what it must be like to have parents who were home with you instead of in jail or passed out on the bed.

He'd had his sister, but they'd had to tiptoe around. When their mother wasn't shouting in a drunken rage, she'd been asleep and they'd done their best to keep her that way.

Law enforcement and the military had been sources of rich friendships, but most everyone else had had families of their own. Sundays had been the worst, he remembered. Sundays were family days and he didn't have anyone to share those days with.

He hoped that when the day came for the truth, Gusty would understand that he wasn't going to be able to let this family go.

As they sat around after dinner drinking more coffee, Brandon and Brady shouted from the other end of the room. "Look! Aunt Gusty's on TV!"

Everyone turned toward the television where the old news story of Gusty's disappearance, now familiar to everyone but Bram and Gusty, was shown again with the update of her rescue by a private firm hired by her brothers-in-law.

"She's now home safe and sound," the newscaster said, "with her sisters and her husband and the baby that was born right after the agents moved in."

Details of Bram's involvement in the Mendez case and Ramon Mendez's attempt on Gusty's life, "finally provided answers to the question we've all been asking for weeks. 'What happened to Augusta Ames?'"

Chatter followed among the anchors about everyone's delight that the story had a happy ending.

The family applauded. Bram joined in, hoping he'd still be applauding when Gusty herself finally knew the whole story.

Chapter Eight

Sadie was a miracle. Gusty was even beginning to believe that her past didn't matter, if her future would be filled with this beautiful baby and Bram.

Now ten days old, Sadie often stared at Gusty while nursing, little fingers opening and closing, legs kicking, toes curling. Gusty thought it very discerning of her baby to find her mother fascinating.

But Sadie seemed even more taken with her father. He talked to her as though she were ten and walking beside him instead of going everywhere in the crook of his arm.

"This is the Quicken program," he told her the day before as they sat together at the kitchen table, his laptop open to his business files. "It's a great thing for those of us who aren't very good at math. Of course, you'll probably be good at everything. Girls test just as high as boys do in national programs, you know."

Gusty's heart swelled with love and gratitude. Five brief weeks ago she'd surfaced from a murder attempt in the Columbia River, and today she had a husband, a child and a generous, loving family.

She was going to stop worrying about the past. If it came, that would be wonderful, a blessing. If it didn't, she could live without it. The here and now was all she needed.

The OB-GYN her sisters had recommended told her what to expect of herself in the first month after birth, and as far as Gusty could tell, she was right on track, even ahead of most.

The pediatrician agreed that Sadie shone among her peers. Gusty was sure her eyes and little limbs moved in a way that anyone would find superior to all other children.

And she was delighted to find herself in the fifty percent of women who felt wonderful after childbirth, and experienced none of the postpartum depression and mood swings common to many.

She was sore, tired easily, though she did feel stronger every day, and found it demoralizing that her maternity clothes didn't fit all that badly.

The book assured her that her stomach would flatten in another week or so, but she'd have killed to be able to wear the black jeans Alexis wore, or the woolen stirrups Athena sported with such svelte style and grace.

Bram didn't seem to notice. Of course, he was probably too tired to know his own name. He often got up with her at night to help with Sadie and walked the baby if she fussed so Gusty could go back to sleep.

In the two-hour intervals of silence, they lay curled up like spoons, Gusty wrapped in his arms.

With Sadie in a soft baby carrier Gusty wore in the front, she mixed together the ingredients for meat loaf, thinking it ironic that she'd wondered just a week ago if their sleeping together would be difficult for Bram. The truth was, it was becoming difficult for her.

For a woman who should be experiencing zero sex drive, she lay quietly in Bram's arms every night while he slept, acutely aware of every place their bodies were in contact, of her own response to his touch, of wanting more.

Yearning desperately for more.

She sighed, dropping the meat loaf mixture into a glass pan and molding it into a loaf shape. She had a month to go before she could do anything at all about her feelings.

Bram, on the other hand, seemed to be experiencing no discomfort, and she couldn't help but wonder, despite his claims of attraction, if she was just not as appealing in their real life as she'd been when they were in danger.

Which led her back to her original concern about just what it was that was wrong between them.

The front door closed and Bram's voice called quietly, "Gus?"

"We're in the kitchen," she called, covering the pan of meat loaf with plastic wrap.

She dismissed all concerns from her mind as he walked into the kitchen. They were foolish and didn't matter, figments of her confusion over her memory loss.

What mattered was now, and she couldn't have asked for a more loving, caring man in her life.

He came to stand behind her and kissed her cheek, leaning over her to look into Sadie's face. The baby responded with a wide-eyed stare, her little pink mouth in an O through which her tiny tongue worked in mysterious movements.

"I'm glad you're teaching her to make meat loaf," he said, kissing Sadie's forehead. "If you do go back to teaching, when will she be ready to cook?"

She had to give her work some serious thought, she knew, but she was already so in love with Cliffside and this apartment with its magnificent view of the ocean that she couldn't imagine herself anywhere else. But maybe that would all change when she remembered.

"She's catching on fast," Gusty said, putting the pan in the refrigerator. "How are things at your office?"

"Dusty," he replied. "I just made a deal with Dotty for housekeeping services. I have a raft of messages I should return, but I can do that later. I was just thinking that it's a beautiful sunny day and we probably won't get many more of them. Want to take the baby out and walk around Dancer's Beach?"

She was pleasantly surprised at that suggestion. "Do you have time to do that?"

"Sure. But wear something warm and bundle up the baby. The breeze off the ocean is cold."

She'd have thought of that, but it pleased rather than annoyed her that he had, too.

Half an hour later, she secured Sadie into the car seat in the back of Bram's Jeep, while he loaded the diaper bag and the stroller frame to which the seat would attach.

"I guess I'll have to start looking for a serious car," he said, as they drove down to the stop sign at the bottom of the driveway. "One more child and we'll be short of room. Are you comfortable?"

"I'm fine. It makes me feel as though I'm on safari, or something. You maintain it well. It looks new."

He laughed as he turned onto the road to town. "That's thanks to Athena and David."

"How come?"

"Seems while we were missing, Athena came looking for you and stayed with David. He went off without her one morning, letting her sleep in, and she decided to go exploring on her own. She found the Jeep keys in the kitchen, and took off with it."

"And?"

"And she got into an accident. The Jeep went down on its side. Dave had it repaired and repainted."

Gusty grinned. "It's nice to know Athena can be a little reckless. She seems too together."

"Dave said she was worried about you and not concentrating as she should have been."

"You're very lucky in your friends," she said sincerely.

He nodded without hesitation. "Yes, I am."

They found a parking spot near the park, assembled

the infant seat-stroller for the first time with just a little fumbling, stashed the diaper bag on the bottom rack, then looked at each other on the sun-dappled street as though they'd accomplished something wonderful.

"This is our first official walk as a family," she said, then laughed. "At least with Sadie on the *outside,* so she can enjoy the view, too."

"Right. We'll have to celebrate with a mocha when we get to the coffee bar in the hotel."

"Yum." She reached for the stroller bar but he brushed her hand away. "I'll push. You just relax and window-shop."

Gusty looked around her at the rich green of the park, the trees now rusty red and gold, at the old and new buildings that lined the main street, the church steeple and the big clock on city hall.

While technically nothing was familiar, the small-town warmth and charm touched something inside her that somehow made it feel like home. This was the kind of town that nurtured people, sheltered them, helped launch them on their way to somewhere else, or enfolded them in its neighborly embrace if they stayed.

She pointed to an Italianate structure across the street. It had a large double-door entrance topped by a theater marquee, with a series of archways on either side of it. Blue chase lights declared it to be the Bijou Theater.

"I *love* to go to the movies," she said. "I wonder

what's pl—'' Then she realized suddenly that, however small, that was a memory.

She socked Bram in the arm. "I love the movies! Did you hear that?"

He pretended pain and rubbed his arm. "Yes, thank you, though why that means I deserve a punch, I don't know."

She held his arm in both of hers. "It was an affectionate attack. Come on."

They crossed the street so that she could get a closer look at the building. A sign in the doorway listed all the building's tenants.

"McGinty's Photos!" she read aloud the names she recognized. "Athena Hartford, Attorney-at-Law! My gosh. It's practically a family affair."

"Trev's is a storefront downstairs," he said. "I'm not sure where Athena's is."

"Hey!" Trevyn stepped out onto the sidewalk and came toward them. "I saw you guys walk across the street. What's going on?" He squatted down in front of the stroller to admire Sadie, who had fallen asleep.

"We're just taking advantage of the sunshine," Bram replied. "Want to join us for a mocha?"

He stood and shook his head regretfully. "Sorry. I have clients due any minute. But I'll take a rain check. You know, I can't believe anyone as funny looking as you could have fathered this beautiful baby. You look like King Kong and Sadie looks like Michelle Pfeiffer must have as a baby."

Bram turned to Gusty and asked flatly, "What was that you said about me being lucky in my friends?"

"Well, hello!" From up the street, a plump older woman approached them in the company of a tall, paunchy man. "I saw Athena yesterday, and she told us they'd found you!"

"Hey, Peg!" Trevyn drew Gusty closer to the couple. "These are the clients I was just telling you about, Peg and Charlie McKeon. Peg, Charlie, this is Augusta Ames. Ah, Bishop," he corrected quickly at a look from Bram. "Gusty Ames Bishop."

"Well, thank you." Gusty extended her hand, then realized the woman didn't have a free hand with which to take it. Between them, she and her husband carried what appeared to be a carousel animal—but it was a rabbit, rather than a horse. And looked a little like the famous, fictional Harvey on amphetamines.

His eyes were wide, his ears at an odd angle, whiskers made out of wire were bent crazily, and there appeared to be a bite taken out of his tail.

The woman put her side of Harvey down and embraced Gusty. "Well, welcome home! Oh, and you had the baby!" She leaned over to look at the still sleeping Sadie. "Isn't she adorable?" she whispered to Charlie.

"She is." The man smiled warmly and, balancing Harvey against his hip, offered his hand. "Our kids have a house here that we're borrowing for a few months while they're busy working. Did you ever get your egg whip?"

Gusty blinked at him. "How did you know I was looking for an egg whip?" As he began to reply, she wondered with surprise, 'How did *I* know I was look-ing for an egg whip?'

"We met Athena when she was looking for the egg whip in the antiques shop," Charlie said. "She held one up to ask Peg if it was the right thing. We were there to buy a lamp. Later we met Alexis because we spoke to her in the coffee bar, thinking she was Athena. You three can really confuse a body!"

He smiled at Bram. "You must be the missing friend. The detective."

"Charlie McKeon," Trevyn said, introducing the two men. "Bram Bishop."

Bram shook his hand. "You need someone to track down the rest of your carousel, Mr. McKeon?"

Charlie laughed. "Peg and I love antiques. We have no idea where to put this, but we couldn't pass it up. It's from a Chester Brinkman carousel. He wasn't as famous as Gustav Dentzel, and had a more whimsical approach, but is a collectible name all the same. The kids will love it."

Gusty doubted it, but they were so enthused about the piece, she couldn't disparage it.

"Gifts are always such a wonderful surprise," she said.

As they talked, a small white station wagon pulled up to the curb. The driver honked.

"Oh!" Peg waved. "There's Dori! We thought we'd walk to town today, but then we found this rab-bit, so I called our daughter from the shop to take it home for us while we meet with Trevyn. She's staying with us for a couple of weeks.'' She beckoned to her.

The driver parked the car and climbed out.

"She's *single*," Peg said in a whisper, "but don't mention it. She tends to blow up."

Charlie shook his head. "Sometimes, Peg, you could make pudding blow up."

Peg frowned at him in hurt surprise. "I just want her to be happy."

"She's happy," he said under his breath, "when you *accept* that she's single."

As he spoke, a very pretty dark-haired young woman came toward them. Peg went to link arms with her and draw her toward the group.

Gusty watched her jealously. In plum-colored sweater and pants, she was another svelte little body with no tummy and a dancer's thighs. She wasn't going to like her.

"Dori, I'd like you to meet some new friends," Peg said. "Gusty and Bram Bishop. And this is our photographer, Trevyn McGinty. Trevyn and Bram used to be CIA agents together."

Dori's eyes widened as she shook hands. "Really?"

"Yes, and Gusty has a very exciting story you might want to listen to one day. Everyone, this is our daughter, Dorianne McKeon. She has a master's degree in English Literature."

Dori looked slightly embarrassed by her mother's last remark.

"I'll bet it isn't everyone," she said, "who makes

introductions with name *and* education. At least she
leaves out weight.''

"Thank goodness for that!" Gusty said feelingly.
She pointed to Sadie in the stroller. "This is our
daughter, Sadie. She's ten days old, so you can imagine why I wouldn't want to be introduced by weight,
either.''

Dori's dark eyes scanned the length of Gusty in her
leggings and big sweater and frowned in puzzlement.
"You look wonderful to me. And what a pretty
baby!" She leaned over to touch the baby's tiny hand
resting on a pink blanket wrapped around her.

Gusty decided that she liked Dori after all.

Dori straightened, then looked doubtfully at the
rabbit. "Mom, where are you going to put that?"

"I thought it'd be fun in one of the children's
rooms," Peg said. "Or on the porch with a welcome
sign on it. What do you think?"

Gusty saw a familiar concern in Dori's eyes. Harvey had the potential to frighten little children and
repel guests.

But she finally nodded and smiled. "I'm sure
there's just the right spot for it. I'll put my back seat
down.''

Trevyn and Bram carried the rabbit and placed it
carefully in the back of Dori's wagon.

"You want to come with us," Peg asked Dori as
Trevyn closed the hatch door, "to scout out sites for
an outdoor shot for our family photo?"

"You're sure an outdoor shot is a good idea?"
Dori asked, turning to Trevyn. "I mean, it is October

on the Oregon Coast and you're going to have seven adults, five children and babies, and a dog. I can imagine you finally getting us all organized just as the sky opens up and drenches our red-and-white outfits.''

Peg turned to Gusty. ''She's a smart girl but sadly lacking in a sense of adventure. Bookish, you know.''

''No,'' Trevyn disputed with a smile at Dori. ''It's a legitimate concern. But if we shoot at the beach, we'll be near a covered picnic area. If we use the park and the trees, there's a shelter there, too.''

Dori nodded. ''I was just asking. Well, you guys have a good time, I've got to go home and get back to work. Nice to meet you, Mr. and Mrs. Bishop, Mr. McGinty.''

Bram and Gusty waved as she climbed into the car and drove away.

Peg watched her go and shook her head. ''I don't know where we went wrong with that girl.''

Charlie groaned. ''We didn't go wrong. She followed three overachiever brothers and one brother none of us could quite let go of even though we lost him. And she's never going to be able to love a man until she knows where she fits.''

''She's a brilliant girl with a loving family. What more does she need to know?''

''It's her life. She has to decide that.''

Peg folded her arms, looking determined. ''Well, I've never been one to stand idly by while...''

Charlie caught her arm and turned her toward

Trevyn's studio. "Don't even finish the thought, Peg. You're not interfering."

"Well, Bram's a detective. He could find Salvatore if we hire—"

"No."

"But if he knew—"

"No. And I'm sure Sal knows everything about Dori. When he thinks it's time to make his move, he will."

Peg sagged visibly. "What if he's found someone else."

Charlie sighed philosophically, though he looked regretful. "Those are the breaks, Peg. And Dori knew it when *she* walked away from him."

There was a long moment of silence, the McKeons staring each other down, Trevyn, Bram and Gusty sharing a look of confusion.

Trevyn pointed to a new indigo-blue truck with the name of his studio on the side in silver letters. "Why don't you two hop into my truck, and we'll go scout out the beach site I had in mind, see what you think."

He unlocked the passenger side door. Charlie helped Peg, then climbed in after her.

Trevyn waved at Bram and Gusty. "Next time you come to town, I'll show you the studio. You have to see the mural Alexis painted for me."

"Deal," Bram promised. "See you later."

Trevyn drove away with a parting tap of the horn.

"Poor Dori," Gusty said as they continued up the street. "I wonder who Salvatore is."

"Obviously someone who cared about her," Bram replied.

"I wonder what he did to her."

Bram wrinkled his brow. "Maybe she did something to him. If her mother would like to get him back in Dori's life, my guess is he's not the one at fault."

Gusty bobbed her head from side to side, considering that. "Why would Dori have walked away if he was so perfect?"

"Women do it all the time," Bram replied. "Yearn for power or independence, or the luxury of making all decisions without having to consider anyone else, and walk away from good relationships."

Walk away from good relationships.

As the words echoed in Gusty's thoughts, she had that flash of memory again of an argument she'd had with Bram and his declaration that she could not take the baby and walk away from him.

This time she saw her own face. She was crying. She was in terrible emotional pain. She felt her own desperation.

And she saw the fury in Bram's face, felt his vise-like grip on her arm.

She screwed her eyes shut and tried to think back to what had precipitated the argument. What? What?

Suddenly she could see all of herself. She wore a tailored gray plaid jumper and a white round-neck blouse much like the one she'd dismissed at the Mathews Mercantile in Paintbrush.

And she was very pregnant. So it had been a recent

argument. Probably just before she'd ended up in the river.

In her mind's eye, her gaze swung to Bram's angry face and she heard him demand, "How could you think so little of me? How could you have done that to us? How can you think I'd let you do *this?*"

The tension between them was high, their anger palpable. She could feel her own misery.

"Oh, God," she whispered as Bram leaned over her solicitously. "What did I do?"

BRAM KNEW by her unfocused but horrified expression that she'd remembered something. He struggled against an ever-encroaching panic.

He put an arm around her as people walked past them. "What do you mean?" he asked gently. "Did you remember something?"

She nodded, her eyes still focused on it and not him. "I remembered it the other day when I made the cell phone call to Athena. I remember arguing with you, and I was at least seven months along, so it must have happened just before I lost my memory. But I can't remember what we were fighting about. I just know I was going to leave you, wasn't I?" She looked up at him then, worry darkening her eyes. "Wasn't I?"

If he replied carefully, he thought, he could get them through this without losing everything. But it was a veritable minefield.

"Yes, you were," he replied.

"Why?"

He pointed to the coffee shop visible a short distance away on the ground floor of the Buckley Arms. "Let's go sit down. You're going to need some caffeine for this."

And placing their order would buy him a little time to compile as much truth as he could for a story that would make sense. And still save his hide.

By the time he'd stood in line behind two other customers, waited for two double mochas, then found Gusty at a small table in a corner with a window that looked out onto the street, he thought he had it.

Sadie, bless her, continued to sleep in the stroller placed between their two chairs.

"You hated my being gone so much on cases. My job requires a lot of time away."

She was frowning at him in concentration and nodding as though that made sense to her.

He went on cautiously.

"I'd just wrapped up the Mendez case when you came out to the Shelldrake to meet me for my...my birthday."

"Yes?"

"They'd already brought him in, but I had to go back for a deposition and you were terrified that something would happen to me. The case had gotten a lot of publicity and every story written about it seemed to feature a roundup of their ruthless past exploits. And, of course, there was a quote or two about threats on my life. You asked me to quit the business, and I said no."

She put a hand to her forehead as though trying to remember that, then dropped it to the table in exasperation. "Why can't I remember that?" she asked anxiously. "It was critical to our lives and our marriage and I..."

He caught her hand and held it, rubbing his thumb soothingly over her knuckles.

"It's all right. It doesn't matter now. You told me you were leaving, that you couldn't stand the worry and the pressure another minute and you didn't want the baby to have a father who was always putting himself in danger."

She shook her head, as though she couldn't believe that of herself. "But I knew what you did when I married you."

He squeezed her hand. "I'm sure that time was worse than you'd expected. It was worse than *I'd* expected. But it's all right. Fate took a hand just as you left me in a huff. When Mendez had me followed, he realized that you were my wife and tried to hurt me by getting rid of you. He actually saved our relationship rather than tearing it apart as he'd hoped to do."

She frowned, thinking hard. "In what I can see of the argument, you said to me, 'How could you have done that to us? How can you do this?'"

He nodded, as though he remembered it as she did.

"Well, I understand the last question. You meant, how could I leave you. That's clear. But what did you mean by 'How could you have done that to us?'" She met his eyes, her own betraying fear of the answer. "What had I done?"

He laughed lightly, as though it was of no consequence. "You ripped our wedding picture out of your wallet and tore it in half. Nothing that awful, but I was in a temper and terrified that you really did intend to leave, so everything seemed bigger than it was.''

She sagged a little in her chair, as though relieved. ''You're sure?''

''I'm sure.''

''I didn't do anything else?''

''No.''

''Because…why didn't I tell my sisters we were married? That we were going to have a baby? Unless I was feeling…I don't know…ashamed, or something. I mean, that's pretty selfish. And I'm wondering if I've done something selfish to you?''

He leaned toward her across the table, catching the back of her head in his palm to bring her closer for a kiss of comfort.

He'd thought her actions selfish once, but he'd had a lot of time to think about it since and decided that her motives were generous, even if her behavior hadn't been.

''Let it go for now,'' he said quietly. ''All you did was tear up a picture.''

''I'm sorry.'' Then she asked on sudden impulse, ''Do you have one in your wallet?''

''What?''

''Our wedding picture.'' She sat up eagerly. ''I'd love to see it. Maybe it'd help me remember.''

His heart threw itself against his ribs. ''Ah, no, I don't.'' He dug his wallet out of his hip pocket. ''But I have one of us taken at the Legion dance in Pansy Junction.''

He handed it across the table to her. In the photograph, she wore the sparkly blue dress he'd told her about, and he wore a suit he'd had to buy in Pansy Junction for the occasion. A women's club had taken photographs at the dance as a fund-raiser. He'd kept the image of the two of them during the long, dark months of wondering why she'd changed her mind about the wedding.

She brought the photo close to her face and a touchingly wistful smile curved her lips. "We look so happy," she observed in a near whisper.

"We usually are," he said.

She sighed and handed back the photo. "So, you don't hate me about the fight?"

He ignored the sudden prick of guilt and smiled. "Do I act like a man who hates you?"

She relaxed and caught his hand. "No, you don't. And I appreciate that. I can't imagine what I was thinking."

He shrugged. "Maybe when you remember everything, you'll decide you had cause."

She linked her fingers with his. "Three weeks before we can make love to each other seems like an eternity," she said with that same wistful smile.

The fact that it was on her mind filled his with wild fantasies. The guilt tried to intrude, but he pushed it away. He'd waited what felt like a lifetime for her to want him again.

"I thought we had to wait six weeks," he said, trying to make it sound as though he had all the patience in the world.

"I've read four to six, so I thought we could compromise with five. I feel wonderful."

He kissed her hand still linked with his. "You look wonderful."

She pulled a wry face. "Large and wonderful. And speaking of which, you want to go buy some pumpkins?"

He had to shift mental gears. "Pumpkins?"

"They're everywhere, haven't you noticed?" She pointed to the coffee shop's counter with its three carved pumpkins, and the tiny pumpkins and straw flowers in the middle of every table. "Halloween's coming. And I probably make a great pumpkin pie, don't I?"

"We haven't been together through fall and Christmas," he said truthfully, "but I'm sure you do."

"I love Christmas," she said.

That was another discovery about herself, but she arched an eyebrow over it. "Now is that a memory, or is it just safe to assume that everyone loves Christmas?"

"I don't," he said. "For most of my life I've been alone for it. A church sent us food and treats once, and a stuffed bear for my sister and a toy truck for me. Of course I was thirteen at the time and thought a truck was lame."

Gusty leaned toward him, her eyes filled with promise. "We are going to have the best holiday you've ever had," she whispered. Then she paused to calculate. "And on the seventh of November, I'm going to make love to you until you're crazy!"

If ever there'd been something to live for...

Chapter Nine

When they headed home, the Jeep looked as though it had swallowed an entire patch of pumpkins. They were everywhere in the back, except for the small space occupied by Sadie's infant seat. Bram had to tie the frame of the stroller to the roof. The diaper bag was wedged in at Gusty's feet and she held a thirty-two-pound pumpkin in her lap.

"And what are we going to do with all these?" he asked as they turned up the driveway to Cliffside.

"Decorate," she said. "Create holiday atmosphere. The smaller, really orange pumpkins I bought in the produce section are for making pies. Or soup. Have you ever had pumpkin soup?"

He winced. "I have to admit it doesn't really appeal to me. Is it coming up on our menu?"

"It is. And I'll change your mind about it."

"Do you remember making pumpkin soup?"

She nodded. "I think I served it to my students in individual bowls made of small pumpkins." She smiled suddenly. "They loved it."

"Do you remember them?"

She shook her head. "Just as a sort of mass—a feeling of excitement and happiness." She sighed and cast him a philosophical glance. "I guess that'll do for now."

"You can't go wrong with happiness and excitement." He parked the Jeep by the back steps. "You take the baby up and I'll make the thirty or so trips with your pumpkins."

She grinned at him. "I don't remember that you're a whiner."

He leaned into the back to unfasten the car seat from its mounting and pass it to her so that she could take it by the handle. "Whining usually earned me a kiss and a very solicitous 'Poor baby!'"

"Oh," she said, kissing his cheek, "Well, you have to tell me these things." She kissed him again and added a heartfelt "Poor baby!"

"Wow!"

"Look at all those pumpkins!"

Brandon and Brady, who'd been shooting hoops, came running at the sight of treasure inside the open back door of the Jeep. Ferdie leaned into it to sniff.

"We don't have our pumpkin yet," Brady said. "We're going tomorrow."

"Tell you what." Bram handed each boy a pumpkin. "You help me carry these upstairs, and you can each have the pumpkin of your choice."

They raced ahead, the dog following and barking ecstatically at the rush of activity.

"Don't run on the stairs!" Gusty shouted after

them, but her caution fell on deaf ears. She followed with the baby.

The next week was a domestic paradise. Bram made himself go to the office and line up cases. He didn't want to, but he was afraid if he was at the apartment all day, Gusty would begin to remember more and more, particularly since she'd recalled the argument.

So far she had no recollection of what surrounded it, but he knew that was just a matter of time.

When he came home at night, she always had dinner ready, something hearty and delicious and so aromatic it enraptured him as he walked up the stairs.

She'd put different-sized pumpkins on every other step going up to the apartment. Inside were smaller ones that remained uncarved but decorated with fall leaves and pyracantha berries she'd found at the florist.

She'd given one to Alexis that Saturday when they'd all helped Trevyn and Alexis move. Lex had stayed at the new house to direct the movers, and Gusty, with Sadie in her baby harness, had prepared meals and kept the coffeepot full.

At ten-thirty that night, when they'd finished, she served pumpkin pie with ice cream and spiced apple cider.

Bram expected the cider to be sweet and unpalatable, but found it delicious instead.

"How come she got all the cooking skills?" David, sitting on the floor and leaning against the sofa, asked an exhausted Athena. She lay on her back on the carpet, her head on his thigh.

Brandon and Brady watched television in a corner of the room, glassy eyed, Ferdie asleep between them, exhausted from a long day of barking.

"I don't know." Athena didn't sound at all repentant. "She makes a great pie, but she wouldn't have been able to handle your legal affairs."

"And great Monte Cristos, and chocolate coconut cookies, quiche…I mean, even Dotty doesn't make quiche for breakfast."

"I heard that!" Dotty shouted from the kitchen, standing on a ladder and organizing dishes in the cupboards. "You all never appreciated fancy things until she started making them." She emphasized the 'she' scornfully, but with a wink in Gusty's direction. "I think the thrill of it is that you don't have to pay her."

Alexis lay sideways in an overstuffed chair, her head on its arm, her legs dangling off the other side.

"I think you guys are fascinated with her because she looks more delicate than Athena and I."

Trevyn, rooting through his camera bag on the floor, cast a questioning glance in her direction. "That's ridiculous. You're all identical."

Athena wagged her index finger back and forth to express a negative. "Feature by feature, yes, but she's always been the sweet one and it's somehow apparent. I come off as competent, Lex as…" She hesitated over the right word.

"Careful," Lex cautioned.

Athena finally settled on "Artistic. Sexy."

"Okay," Alexis said. "That's not bad."

"But Gusty makes you want to fuss over her, take care of her, even though she's perfectly competent and as artistic as Lex in her own way."

"It's because I was born last." Gusty sat in Bram's lap in another large chair, the baby in her arms. "You think of me as the youngest, and have passed on that attitude to the men, that's all."

"And you're a better cook than either of them," David insisted. "Trev, Bram and I ate major garbage on some of our jobs, and for long periods. So we'll go a long way to protect the woman who prepares delicious food."

"Ha!" Dotty cried from the kitchen.

"Didn't I say you weren't home," David asked, "when the produce buyer at Coast Groceries wanted to ask you out?"

"True," Dotty replied. "And I'll be eternally grateful for that."

Lexie sat up properly in the chair. "Isn't that Benjamin?"

David nodded.

"But he's such a nice man. Why don't you want to go out with him, Dotty?"

"Because I don't need a man."

"What about a friend?"

"Men don't want friends, they want women!"

"Whoa!" Trevyn cried, getting to his feet and turning the rewind lever on his camera. "That's a sexist remark if I ever heard one."

"True," Bram said under his breath, "but sexist."

Gusty bit his earlobe as everyone laughed.

"Ow!" he complained halfheartedly. "Nice example for your daughter."

"Men want someone who understands them," David said. "Just like women do. Or, at least, someone willing to try."

"But I'm set in my ways," Dotty said, peering at them between the cupboards and the counter. "And I like doing just exactly what I want to do."

"But that's just existing," Gusty countered, "not living."

Everyone turned to her in surprise. "That was profound," Bram teased.

She smiled with embarrassment. "That's because Benjamin helped me find just the right baking pumpkins," she said, pointing to the empty pie plate on the coffee table. "And when I told him I lived at Cliffside, he said he's always wanted to get to know our housekeeper better."

"Oh, no," Dotty said in a small voice.

Gusty nodded. "I'm afraid so. I invited him to our Halloween party and promised to arrange a dance between the two of you."

Dotty groaned and sat down on the top of the ladder.

"What harm can one dance do?" Trevyn asked, focusing the camera on her. She had her face buried in her hands. He snapped the shutter.

Dotty gave him a dirty look.

"You dance, you chat, then you know if it's anything worth pursuing." He turned the camera toward

Alexis, who was back in her legs-over-the-side position. "That's how I got Lex, you know."

She put a pillow over her face. "You let me go after we danced," she said.

"No, I didn't," he disputed, focusing and shooting. "You ran away. Take the pillow down. I want a record of our house, starting with the exhaustion of moving in."

"I had to run away," she said, tossing the pillow aside and pointing one leg in a balletic pose. "It was Athena's plan to learn the truth about all of you and have you arrested for stealing our inheritance from us."

Gusty, relaxed in Bram's arms, got a sudden image of her and her sisters standing in front of Cliffside in the rainy, chill night air, waiting for someone to answer the door. Athena had been dressed like a Jane Austen character, Alexis like a flapper, and she...she'd been a Southern belle. And she'd been terrified that she wouldn't be able to pull off the deception.

She heard the click of Trevyn's camera, felt the flash of a light.

"I remember that," she said.

Everyone turned in her direction.

"What do you remember?" Athena asked, sitting up.

Gusty relayed what she'd just seen in her mind. "I was scared," she said. "Afraid I could never be that appealing that a man would tell me his secrets."

IRONIC CHOICE OF WORDS, Bram thought. She was lying in his arms, so he struggled to appear calm.

"And now you know all of mine," he said, kissing the top of her head.

She leaned into him contentedly. "I guess you're safe until I can remember them myself."

She didn't know just how true that was.

"Things are starting to come back?" Athena asked.

"Yeah." Gusty sounded tired, as though the entire subject had made her bone weary. "Just flashes, pictures, like what Trevyn's taking. Just glimpses and moments, no sequence to tell me what it all means."

Trevyn turned to David and Athena seated on the floor. "I'm sure that'll be next," he said, focusing on them and shooting. "Try not to worry over it. Because of our experience in Afghanistan, I had a sort of confusion of events, things overlapped so that I didn't know what happened when. But the less I worried over it, the clearer it got."

"I know that makes sense," she said. "And I thought I'd decided to do that. But the more I see of Athena and Alexis, the more I want to remember what we've shared, what Aunt Sadie was like, the love Bram and I had for each other that brought our baby into being." She sighed against him, almost listless as she spoke. "I try to be patient, but the wanting to know sometimes beats me down."

Alexis sat up again and leaned her body toward them, though she sat across the room. "But the holidays are coming, and you've always loved them. You're the one who fussed the most, baked and crafted and shopped, and sent Sadie and Athena and me things in the mail every other day from our 'holiday angel.' I'll bet it all comes rushing back to you when you put up your tree. You have a lot of ornaments from our childhood, ornaments Sadie sent you from her travels and old things you've collected on your own.''

''Speaking of old things,'' Gusty said, ''we met Charlie and Peg McKeon today, and Peg asked me if I ever got my egg whip.''

''Oh!'' Athena sprang to her feet and sprinted to the kitchen. ''That's right! I keep forgetting to give it to you!''

Ferdie looked up, then deciding his services weren't required, went back to sleep.

Gusty sat up, put the baby in the crook of Bram's arm and slid off his lap to join Athena. Alexis followed.

''Dotty,'' Athena began, ''there was a box marked Gus—''

''Over there by the toaster.'' Dotty pointed toward the window over the sink. ''I put it aside, intending to ask you what I was supposed to do with it.''

Trevyn closed in with the camera as Athena handed Gusty the box. Gusty opened it, then emitted a sound of pleasure as she took a strange-looking object made of what appeared to be coiled wire in the shape of the bowl of a spoon. It was attached to a handle.

She held it up and her sisters leaned in for a closer look.

Trevyn snapped one picture after the other, completely unnoticed by his subjects.

Gusty made a rotary motion with the object. "You use it to whip eggs, just like a whisk."

"You're coming back to make breakfast, then?" Alexis asked.

Gusty pursed her lips at her. Trevyn snapped the shutter. "No, but you're welcome to come to our place if you don't have the energy to cook. Maybe you'll have to keep Dotty, and David can hire me."

Alexis turned to David. "How about it?"

"Not a chance." He shook his head firmly. "Haven't you noticed that Bram gets all her attention. He'd never let her go. If Dotty went with you, I'd have to depend on Athena's cooking, and you wouldn't wish that on me, would you?"

The evening collapsed into teasing and laughter and they all parted company just after midnight.

"It's not going to seem right without you at Cliffside," Athena said as she hugged Alexis, then Trevyn.

"They're less than half a mile away," David said, putting an arm around Athena's shoulders. "Trev and Bram and I are talking about meeting at the gym every morning before breakfast. The three of you should meet to walk on the beach or something."

"What'll I do while you're all getting buff?" Dotty asked, an arm around each of the boys.

"You'll have Benjamin," Brady said, then frowned at Brandon. "And we'll have school. I can't wait to be an adult so I can go to the gym instead."

David shepherded his group out to his car, Ferdie following with a yawn, as Gusty and Bram said goodbye.

"You know, a morning walk's a good idea," Alexis said, leaning down to kiss Sadie's little head. "We can all take turns pushing the stroller. I'm sure Ferdie would love to come."

Gusty nodded. "I like the idea. Then we can end up at the coffee bar for mochas and pastry."

From the driveway, Brady could be heard complaining, "Did you hear that? We miss *all* the good stuff!"

Sadie was wide-awake when Bram and Gusty climbed the stairs to their apartment. Gusty tried to shoo Bram off to bed.

"I have to feed her," she said. "Why should we both stay up? Get a couple of hours' sleep, then you can get up with her at 2 a.m."

"Tomorrow's Sunday," he replied, going to put on the kettle. "Doesn't matter how late I sleep. You feed her, then I'll burp her when you're finished and you can go to bed."

"I don't think I'll be able to sleep." She yawned, though, as Sadie settled at her breast. "I keep getting these flashes of things. It doesn't tell me much, but it keeps me from relaxing."

"I think we can fix that." He ignored what that meant to him, and tried to think only of what it meant to her.

"How?"

He wedged himself into the space she'd left between herself and the arm of the sofa, then turned her slightly and leaned her against his chest. Sadie continued to nurse as though God himself could not have pulled her free.

"Now you're going to fill me with lustful images instead," she said, but she relaxed her weight against him with a satisfied sigh. "That won't help me sleep, either."

He laughed, cupping his hand around Sadie's head.

"That's good. You keep those lustful images forward in your mind. Experiment with them so that when the three weeks are up, we'll make up for lost time."

"Yeah," she whispered and promptly fell asleep.

RAIN FELL IN TORRENTS two days before Halloween. Gusty and her sisters were gathered in the kitchen at the big house, preparing for the party. While Dotty and Gusty rolled out pastry dough for hors d'oeuvres, Athena and Alexis hollowed out pumpkins and filled them with bouquets of dried leaves. Ferdie was asleep under the table.

The men were in the garage, tying cornstalks into bundles.

"Where did you get cornstalks?" Athena asked Gusty. She wore a functional white apron and an uncharacteristically mussy air. But Gusty thought she seemed to be having fun. "It's not like the Oregon Coast is farm country."

"Coast Groceries," Gusty replied with a smiling glance at Dotty. "Benjamin was anxious to help me.

I think he had them brought down from Brownsmead near Astoria.''

Dotty frowned back. "I suppose you sold me into sexual slavery to get them?''

"You don't mind, do you?'' Gusty asked with all apparent seriousness. "We need the cornstalks for atmosphere.''

"Of course not,'' Dotty replied, cutting her sheet of pastry in half. "Now that you've all found love, you're determined to get rid of me so you can have this kitchen to yourselves. And the best way to do that is to marry me off.'' She pulled toward her a bowl of chopped livers sautéed in wine and began to place the mixture on one half of the pastry. "Well, it isn't going to work. Now that you're all working so hard you'll all be too busy to cook.''

She pointed her spatula at Gusty. "You're the only fly in my ointment. You can do everything I can with one hand tied behind your back and still have time to cover the earth in decorated pumpkins! My only hope is that you'll keep having children and be too busy to stay in the kitchen.''

The thought of having children logically brought Gusty's thoughts around to sex, which reminded her that in a short eight days or so, she and Bram would be able to make love.

She wished she could remember the nights they'd shared. As time approached, she was getting nervous. Had they really been good together? If so, how could she have threatened to leave him when she loved him as she did?

Or had she loved him like this then? Was the totality of her emotions now something that had developed with the subtle changes in her? And if she was a different woman than she'd been when they met, would their lovemaking be the same? Would he still find pleasure in her?

She didn't doubt for a moment that she'd find it in him. Just lying in his arms at night gave her a delicious sense of well-being and made her long for more.

"Hello?" Dotty snapped her fingers in Gusty's face. "You're dreaming of taking my job from me, aren't you?"

Alexis laughed, going to the sink to wash her hands. "No, she's thinking about Bram. Can't you tell by that mushy look on her face? It's been almost a month since she had the baby. Pretty soon it'll be time to set the night on fire."

Gusty blushed. "Yes, it's on my mind all the time. I wasn't a nymphomaniac before I lost my memory, was I?"

Athena laughed. "Quite the opposite. You were very picky where men were concerned. Lex and I didn't even know you had a man in your life, much less a baby on the way."

Gusty picked up a circular pastry cutter to punch round shapes out of her sheet of dough.

"I guess I…" she began, then saw an image in her mind of herself sitting on the steps of her porch in Pansy Junction. A car was driving away.

She felt a great joy and a terrible sadness all curiously entangled. She struggled to concentrate, wondering what could have happened to fuse such opposite emotions.

Love, she realized. She was in love. Her heart was driving away with Bram, who'd just shown up out of the blue after their first, brief encounter at the Cliffside party, and spent four days with her.

At the party, she'd tried to approach him with the woman-of-mystery air she'd known Athena and Alexis would use on his friends to secure information about David's inheritance of the house.

But she had little skill at subterfuge and Bram had charmed her out of her attempt to be mysterious, and soon had her talking about herself.

After a while, she'd told him all about the children in her classroom.

He'd smiled. "I like other people's children," he'd said with a rakish smile under the brim of his Musketeer's hat. "But I don't think I'd care to have my own."

"Why not?" she'd asked, always surprised that someone could live without children.

He'd shrugged. "Bad beginning. A career that doesn't always respect life. I think I've just gotten too...too rough to be trusted with a child's life."

She remembered knowing instinctively how wrong he was about himself, yet understanding how convinced he was that what he said was true.

She'd felt sorry and sad and knew it was time to go. He'd been distracted for a moment by a question from someone else and she'd taken the opportunity to try to run.

But with a lightning reflex, he'd caught her hand.

"I have to go," she'd said.

"And I have to know your name," he'd insisted. When she'd hesitated, he'd added, "Please?"

She'd shaken her head, pulled free and run away. But she knew something about him already. He'd find her.

The sound of Sadie crying brought her out of the memory to the awareness that everyone was staring at her.

"Are you all right? Did you remember something?" Alexis said worriedly.

Her sisters closed in on her as she picked up Sadie from the infant carrier on the counter and put her to her shoulder.

"I remembered my conversation with Bram that night we crashed the party," she said, a curious unease lingering with the foggy remnants of the memory. "He told me he didn't want children."

Athena looked into her face, then guided her toward the small sofa in a little conversation area off the kitchen.

"Are you remembering something else? Here, sit down and just relax."

Alexis pushed a hassock under her feet. "Want me to take the baby? You're holding her a little tightly."

Gusty realized Sadie was screaming, and handed her to Alexis. Something was trying to come back—she saw overlapping impressions that first defied sorting. But there was a grimness to them, and she felt her own instinctive reluctance to try to remember.

Something bad had happened.

Athena sat with her while Alexis walked the baby and Dotty brought a mug of tea.

Gusty was aware of all that while still trying to make herself remember. What had hurt so much? What had been so awful that even now she could feel the pain through an unremembered past.

"Something bad happened," she said, her voice a little thin.

Athena held her hand. "It's all right. We're here. And if it's a memory, it was in the past and you survived it, so you'll survive it again. Let it come."

Dotty took the baby from Alexis, who sat on the other side of her. "Breathe, Gusty," Alexis said gently.

Gusty could see darkness. Herself. She was asleep. Then there was the ring of the telephone.

"Gusty?" a familiar voice said. But it was strained, barely controlled, filled with tears.

Gusty turned to Athena. "You called me," she said.

Athena frowned. "When?"

"I don't know. You were crying." Gusty closed her eyes and heard Athena's voice. "Gus, oh, Gusty. Aunt Sadie had an accident."

Gusty saw herself sit up in bed, panic inching up inside her. "What kind of accident?"

"She was island-hopping in Hawaii in one of those tiny planes and it went down!"

Athena had burst into tears.

"Oh, God," Gusty whispered now, love flooding

back to her, grief overwhelming her. Their mother's sister had given them all her love. She'd cared for them summers and holidays and any other time their presence had been inconvenient for their parents.

"What?" Athena asked.

"Sadie," Gusty replied, tears spilling over, pain kicking around inside her.

Athena wrapped her in her arms. "I know. I'm sorry. It must be awful to feel all that as though it were new." She rubbed Gusty's shoulder as they wept together. "Do you remember that she left you her doll collection? And that antique bear you used to cuddle when we were small?"

She remembered seeing the lineup of dolls when Bram had taken her to Pansy Junction before they'd hidden out in the cabin. But she hadn't realized then how she'd acquired them.

Sadie, Gusty now remembered, had always encouraged her to be her own person, not to worry that she didn't have Athena's brilliance or Alexis's sense of adventure. "You're your own very special person and there's nothing at all wrong with that. Look at me. I'd rather be here at Cliffside than anywhere, sitting in the window, drinking coffee and watching the water."

Of course, that had been a fib, Gusty now knew. Sadie had been a spy—just like Bram, Trevyn and David. They'd known her; that's why she'd left Cliffside to David. Talk about a sense of adventure. She'd gone off to dangerous places and done life-threatening work.

Grief struck her anew, plunged deep. Wrapped together in a tight knot of mutual pain, she and her sisters wept.

Gusty held on to them, mourning Sadie, yet curiously certain there was a part of her grief Sadie didn't occupy.

There was another dark pocket in her memory that had started to open, then closed itself tightly when she remembered Sadie. Her brain's way of protecting her, she suspected.

For now, it would have to rest there, waiting to reveal itself. The way things were coming back to her, it wouldn't be long.

She felt like a bomb with a very short fuse.

Chapter Ten

"I think mine are the most artistic cornstalks in the bunch." Trevyn stood one up against the side of his truck and stepped back against Bram's Jeep to study it. "Look at the perfect lines, the artful..."

"Oh, get over it," David said, snatching it by a stalk and leaning it up against the back of the garage with the others. "It's just a bundle of stalks. Do you think there's any coffee left inside?"

Bram looked out at the driving rain. "I could sure use a cup, but look at that rain." He turned to grin at his friends. "This reminds me of a job I did in Manila. I've never seen so much rain fall so fast."

David came to stand beside him. "You ever regret the decision to leave the CIA?"

Bram was surprised by the question. "No. You?"

David shook his head. "I wondered. We all quit on spur-of-the-moment frustration with everything, then I got this place and dragged you both out here. I just sometimes wonder if you followed me because you really wanted to, or because it was habit."

"Follow you?" Trevyn said, wedging his way between them. "You don't really think of either one of us as a follower, do you? We came because you had a place to live and were willing to support us."

David laughed. "I meant—"

"We know what you meant," Bram interrupted, "and we don't regret coming to Dancer's Beach. It is unfortunate that you were included in the deal, but hey, life is hard. On the other hand, you were strange-looking enough to convince three beautiful women that you'd bilked their aunt out of her home thereby forcing them to crash our party and get to know us for their own evil purposes. So, all in all, I'd say we're in your debt."

"Very astute of you." David pushed both of them out into the rain, then followed them at a run. "Let's get that coffee and see what other chores the rowdy redheads have for us."

Bram, David and Trevyn came to a stumbling halt at the edge of the kitchen. Athena, Alexis and Gusty sat together on the sofa, sobbing. Dotty walked Sadie, who was screeching at the top of her lungs.

"What happened?" Bram went forward to peel Gusty out of the middle of her sisters. "What's the matter?"

David sat beside Athena, Trevyn on the other side of Alexis.

"I just remembered Sadie dying." Gusty wrapped her arms around Bram's neck and held on. "And I guess I started the grief all over again for them. I'm sorry. I'll get it together in a minute."

"It's all right." He drew her aside and rocked her gently. "I'm sure it makes you feel like you did when you heard it the first time."

"She was so good to us. If it hadn't been for her, we wouldn't know what a mother's love was like."

He could relate to that. "She was like an aunt to me and Dave and Trevyn. We never saw her, only talked to her on the radio, but she mothered us, too, besides doing her job as our contact."

"I hope she knows we're happy. I wonder if she left David the house so that we'd be forced to stop thinking of Cliffside as the only place where we could be happy. So that we'd have to look for happiness, or make it happen ourselves."

"It's hard to know what was on her mind." He hugged her tightly, then drew her away and grinned into her tearful eyes. "But if you want her to know you're happy, I think you're going to have to do better than this. Even from some astral plane, I'm sure she's thinking this doesn't look like happiness."

She sighed and seemed to collect herself. Then she became aware of the baby's screeching.

"Oh my gosh!" She turned to Dotty and took the baby from her.

"Why don't you take her home for a nap?" Dotty said. "I can finish the pastries. And you should probably rest after that. It must be very traumatic to have your life come back to you like a series of ambushes."

Gusty was about to protest, but Athena rose from the sofa and ordered, "Go. We can finish up."

David, rising too, smiled at Gusty. "The queen has spoken. Better do as she says, or it'll be hard on the rest of us."

"But we'll expect you back the morning of the party to help us set up." Alexis leaned around Gusty to look into the baby's face. Sadie's screeches had quieted somewhat, but she was still very unhappy. "You'll remember that she wasn't crying when *I* was holding her. Dotty's the one who made her cry."

"She's picking up the sadness in all of you," Dotty said. "She'll be fine when she's home again."

Everyone walked to the door.

"I am sorry I messed up our work party," Gusty said sincerely.

Alexis shrugged. "I wasn't having any fun anyway. I'm going to leave the rest to Dotty and Athena and go shopping."

"You can't do that," Athena said seriously. "I was going to use you for a jack-o'-lantern pattern."

David closed the door on the mayhem that followed.

At the apartment, Gusty fed Sadie, who fell asleep after a healthy belch.

"I'll put her down," Bram said, taking the baby and pointing to the sofa. He wanted Gusty to rest, preferably before she remembered anything more. "You lie down for a while. You look flushed and tired."

Gusty smirked at him. "We'll be tired for the rest of our lives. I wonder how parents get any sleep when they have twins?"

Bram walked toward the bedroom with Sadie. "I don't recommend we find out just yet. Lie down. I'll bring you a pillow."

She pointed to the kitchen. "I have things to…"

He silenced her with a look and pointed to the couch. "Don't make me shout when I'm holding the baby. I'll bring you a pillow, then a cup of tea, and I want you to rest."

He walked into the bedroom, hoping to create the impression that he expected her to cooperate.

But when he returned to the living room, Gusty was in the kitchen. The kettle was going, she had cups down, one containing a tea bag, and she was reaching for the coffee carafe.

He got a certain satisfaction out of her little squeal of surprise as he swept her up into his arms.

"Are you deaf, woman?" he asked with mild impatience. "What did I just say?"

She sighed. "Don't tell me I'm in the habit of doing everything you say?"

"It would be a nice change if you did it even occasionally." He deposited her on the sofa where he'd already tossed a bed pillow.

"But I was—"

"And without a lot of lip," he added, opening the green and yellow throw over her.

"I'm not tired from remembering I'm…just…"

"Just what?" He tucked her in, then leaned an arm on the back of the sofa, waiting for her to answer.

She sighed again. "There's something else," she said cryptically.

"What do you mean?" he asked.

She touched a spot between her breasts. "There's something else besides the grief. Something bad."

Oh, God. He braced himself. "Tell me," he said.

She shook her head. "I don't know what it is. I just know it's there. It has something to do with you and me, I think." She looked him in the eye. "I hurt you somehow."

He smoothed her hair back, worried about the look in her eyes. She was half with him, and half not, as though memory was reclaiming her.

"Do I look as though I'm injured?" he asked.

"No, you don't. But I'm learning that you're very generous."

"Then there's nothing to worry about."

"I can't go ahead," she insisted, "without repairing what I've done."

The kettle whistled. He patted her hand, secretly grateful for the reprieve, and went to make her tea.

He took it to her and found that her eyelids drooped sleepily. "I loved Aunt Sadie," she said, her voice a little thick.

He sat on the edge of the sofa and held her hand. "I know you did. I'm sorry."

"I love our Sadie."

"Yes. I do, too."

"I love our little life here," she continued, her eyelashes fluttering closed.

"I do, too."

She fell asleep on that thought. He resolved with reluctant determination that when she awoke, he would have to tell her the truth. He had to explain the gaps she couldn't remember so that they stopped torturing her, then he had to tell her the truth about their relationship.

But, first, she needed the sleep.

THE EARTH WAS COVERED with fog. It whirled in drifting patterns across a landscape Gusty couldn't identify. She could feel drops of moisture on her face, dampening her hair, chilling her body. But inside, her heart was even colder and it had nothing to do with the fog.

She had a burden. A heavy burden.

The fog parted and she saw her home in the distance. She ran toward it, eager to be warm again. She ran and ran but seemed to make no progress. Her home was as far away as it had seemed when she'd started.

Her burden grew heavier. She tried to shift it, to make the weight more comfortable, but she couldn't because she wasn't carrying it in her arms, but in her body.

It was a baby.

"No," she heard herself cry. "No! No!"

Gusty awoke, still shouting. Bram came from the kitchen, a dish towel over his shoulder, his eyes dark with concern. He sat beside her, pushing the tumbled hair from her face.

She caught his upper arms. Guilt and confusion warred inside her.

"I wanted the baby!" she said anxiously. "I wanted her from the beginning. I did!"

He was frowning. He didn't understand.

"You were having a bad dream," he said quietly. "It was just a dream."

"But in it I saw myself running toward home," she explained urgently. "I was running and running and home kept getting farther and father away. And there was this pressure in my stomach." She winced as though in pain. "It was heavy and hard and some-how…dark."

He nodded. "But it was a dream. It wasn't real."

"But isn't a dream your subconscious dealing with things you don't take care of during the day? Wouldn't that suggest that I didn't *want* Sadie? But I did, didn't I?"

He looked at her for an instant, as though uncertain what to say.

"Bram!" She tightened her grip on his arms. "I wanted her."

"Of course you wanted her," he said quickly. "Dreams don't mean anything, and if they do, we can't interpret them like we do waking thought. It's not the same."

And then like the sudden illumination of a television screen, she saw herself in a doctor's office. She sat on a hospital bed, swinging her bare legs.

The doctor was a balding, middle-aged man she'd known since she'd moved to Pansy Junction. He'd set her arm after a class trip to the skating rink, given her antibiotics for bronchitis, stitched her finger when she caught it trying to fix a faulty pencil sharpener.

But that day she was happy, smiling.

Something relaxed inside Gusty as she watched the picture unfold. She wanted the baby. She did.

The doctor, sitting on a stool on wheels, looked up at her with a somber expression. "The lab report shows alpha-fetoprotein in your amniotic fluid," he said.

She felt her trepidation in the image. She didn't know what that was, but she knew the doctor didn't like it.

She asked questions.

He replied that it suggested a neural tube defect.

She asked what that could mean.

He gave her a terrifying list—Down syndrome, cystic fibrosis, Trisomy 18, a disorder that carried with it mental retardation, a congenital heart defect, and all manner of other abnormalities.

She felt everything inside her freeze.

"I'm sorry, Gusty," the doctor said. "You might want to think about your options."

Her options.

There was no question in her mind about the baby. She loved children. All children. Smart ones, slow ones, beautiful ones…threatened ones.

"I'm having the baby," she said. "What do we do next?"

Gusty, sitting up in the middle of the sofa, clutched Bram's arms as tears filled her eyes.

"I had a bad amniocentesis test," she said, puzzled, newly frightened. "All kinds of things were supposed to be wrong with the baby."

He nodded, turning his hands to hold her arms. "It was a false positive. When you had an ultrasound in your seventh month, she was fine. Everything was fine. The doctor said that just happens sometimes. They'll get a bad reading and everyone expects the worst, until an ultrasound proves otherwise. We were so lucky."

Relief washed over her like a shower. She put a hand to the block in her chest where that dark place lived, waiting for it to disappear, but it didn't.

"Is there a chance she'll develop something later?" she asked Bram.

"No," he said firmly. "She's perfect."

"Then why am I...?"

The image returned with a sudden flash and she saw herself driving home from the doctor's office, making the cold-blooded decision not to tell Bram.

She understood clearly everything that was in her mind that day.

She hadn't told him about the pregnancy yet, because she hadn't seen him since those four days after he'd tracked her down. They talked every other day on the phone, but she'd wanted to be sure everything was perfect before she told him.

Because he'd told her the night they'd met that he didn't want to have children. But many men said that and quickly changed their minds at the prospect of becoming a father. And she'd been confident he would, too.

He had all a good father's qualities—patience, tenderness, a sense of humor, a possessive protectiveness that somehow made her feel more free than she'd ever felt in her life.

But if she'd have had to coax him into accepting his role as father, she doubted that she could do it with a child destined to have serious health problems. And she would not terminate this pregnancy, because whatever happened, she'd conceived this baby in love, and would love it always.

So she would have to terminate her relationship with Bram.

She saw herself on the telephone. "...and I've been thinking that this all happened much too suddenly, got far too serious in much too brief a time. It can't be real. I don't believe it's real. We've made a terrible mistake."

There was a long, loud silence on the other end of the line.

"Bram?" she prompted.

"I'm here," he said finally. "I'm just not believing my ears. Gusty, what's happened?"

She copied her mother's voice; she remembered it well.

"I've just come to my senses, that's all. I'm not in love with you. You're not in love with me."

"I'm coming up tonight," he said.

"I don't want to see you," she'd said coolly. "Please don't come. We were two people in masks, Bram. And with the masks off, well—whatever we thought was there just isn't. Goodbye."

"Gus—"

She'd hung up the phone and wept until she'd been sick.

GUSTY PUT BOTH HANDS to her mouth to stifle a gasp, her eyes wide and dismayed above them.

His heart stalled.

"I called you," she said in a raspy voice, "and told you it was over!"

Just the memory of that call cut the heart right out of him all over again. "Yes, you did."

"Because I thought…"

He nodded, happy for her that her memory was returning—even the painful things—yet fearful for himself because it could mean his days with her were numbered.

"Yeah," he said, holding her hands. "You made a bad decision, but I straightened you out."

"And you stayed." She made the statement in wonder, the love for him always present in her eyes now very bright.

"I did," he said. She hadn't mentioned specifics, so that was true, if not necessarily accurate.

She rubbed her head worriedly. "I can't remember the ultrasound that said the baby was all right."

"I've got it." Now there was a lucky break. "Hold on."

He went to their room, dug in the front pocket of his backpack for his folded-in-four copy of the document and took it to her.

She read it greedily. "Open NTD risk assessment—negative. Down syndrome risk assessment—negative. Trisomy…'' She looked at him in wonder. ''They're all negative. She is fine?''

''You heard Dr. Grayson. She's perfect. And the new pediatrician said so, too.''

She winced. ''I was terrified, then caused you all that anguish…for nothing?''

''Yes,'' he replied. ''And aren't we grateful?'' He spread his arms to indicate their surroundings. ''This is where the three of us are now. Healthy, safe, together.''

She flung her arms around him with an exaggerated groan. ''I feel I could sleep for a week.''

''Why don't you lie down again?''

She shook her head. ''Want to come to the bed with me,'' she asked, ''so we can nap together? I'd really like that.''

''Then you've got it.'' He stood, drew her to her feet and led the way, deciding that the truth could wait until she was rested.

She stripped down to her slip, he to briefs and his T-shirt, and they curled up as they always did, her warm, smooth back against his chest.

Another week, he thought as he tried to distract himself from any feeling below his waist. He could do this.

An hour and a half later he awoke to find her looking into his eyes, her arms folded and leaning on his chest. She looked happy, content. He loved that—and the knowledge that he'd helped put that brightness in her eyes and her smile.

"Do you think we should move into the guest house?" she asked.

Her hair was a wild mass of softly curling red. He reached both hands behind her head to catch it and hold it back.

"Or we could look for our own place," he suggested. "Would you like that?"

She touched her fingertip to his chin. "I hadn't thought of that. I guess from what you've told me, we have a down payment."

"Easily."

"And between our stuff at Pansy Junction, and the things here that are yours, we could furnish one."

"Partially, anyway. We should find something with four or five bedrooms, so we won't have to move again when we decide to test out your twin theory."

She giggled. It sounded youthful and heartwarming and made him very happy.

"Would you like more children?"

"Yes. I think Sadie proves we're brilliant at it."

She turned to gaze lovingly at the crib. "She does, doesn't she? But you must be getting pretty tired of moving. I mean, the three of you left Chicago to come here, then you moved to Pansy Junction when we got married, then we hid out at the cabin, and now we're here. That's a lot of moving in one year."

He nodded, looking away. "That's why this should be our last move. At least until we retire to Coral Gables, or somewhere."

"I love old houses," she said, turning onto her side and resting her head in the hollow of his shoulder.

He held her to him. "Dancer's Beach has quite a few of them. Several on the hill above town. The views must be beautiful."

"And we'll need a yard."

"Definitely."

"And a fence."

"We can put one up if it doesn't have one."

"With climbing roses growing on it," she said dreamily. "Pink ones. And a pergola to walk through from the street."

"One of those trellis things?"

"Yes. Clematis would be pretty, but roses look so homey."

"Then we'll plant roses."

Sadie stirred and started to cry.

"I'm here, baby." Gusty turned and swung her legs out of bed.

Sadie stopped crying before she even reached her, already alerted that the sound of her voice meant rescue. Love was such a miracle.

And Sadie wasn't the only one who appreciated it.

Chapter Eleven

Bram and Gusty dawdled over dinner, Sadie awake and alert in the crook of Bram's arm. She watched the progress of his fork from plate to mouth, then studied him closely while he chewed.

"I get the feeling that she's going to rip this fork out of my hand at any moment," he said, "and polish off the rest of my chicken casserole."

Gusty laughed. "I know. She's getting more and more aware all the time, and more expressive."

And then, as they watched her together, she smiled.

"Did you *see* that?" Gusty demanded, getting out of her chair to lean over them. "She smiled! She smiled at us! She's not supposed to do that for a while yet."

Bram touched her bottom lip with the tip of his index finger, hoping to get her to do it again. But she'd become serious once more—wide, round eyes staring, little mouth forming funny shapes.

"She's obviously the result of superior genetics,"

he said. "Maybe if we wait quietly, she'll tell us what she's smiling about."

Gusty laughed and kissed him soundly. Then she leaned over and kissed the baby's forehead. Bram pulled her down onto his knee and for a few moments they sat all wrapped around each other, absorbing the warmth of their tiny family.

"When I remembered my Aunt Sadie today," Gusty said eventually, "I remembered my childhood, too. My mother. And all I could think about was how much she missed because she wouldn't let us be important to her. For a woman who wanted everything to be about her, she missed a great opportunity when she wouldn't give us any part of herself. When I remember how we loved Aunt Sadie, I think our mother would have considered loving us a bargain if she'd only understood how much she'd get back by giving just a little."

Bram rubbed her back. "I know. My parents never surfaced from their own selfish little worlds long enough to give anything to us but grief. Neither one of them ever saw how special Lisa was. Or how eager I'd have been to be able to connect with either one of them. I didn't even give up the need until I was in high school." He kissed her cheek. "Knowing how important it is to give is a very precious thing."

Gusty tightened the arms wrapped around his neck. "I can't believe I almost let you get away. *Pushed* you away! It's a good thing you're so stubborn."

"Isn't it?" He allowed himself to enjoy another one of her enthusiastic hugs, then opened his mouth to tell her that they had to talk, that there were a few things about the past she wasn't remembering, when she suddenly leaped off his lap, her eyes alight.

"I forgot to show you our costumes for the party!" she exclaimed, heading for the bedroom. "Don't move. I'll be right back."

He bit back the words—shamelessly happy to do so—and waited for her return. He heard stirrings in the bedroom, the rustling of fabric, a squeal of laughter, then she walked out of the bedroom, her slender legs covered in black tights, her torso wrapped in a large, fuzzy black-and-yellow-striped egg-shaped body that covered her from neck to hip. Her arms were covered in the sleeves of a black sweater, and on her head was a bulbous covering in the same black-and-yellow stripe with the added bonus of antennae created by two glittery gold balls bobbing crazily on the ends of long, narrow springs.

She was apparently supposed to be a bumblebee with great legs. She looked adorable.

"Show me your stinger," he asked with the lift of an eyebrow.

She made a face at him. "I don't sting, I just make honey."

He caught her hand and drew her closer. "How come I'm not getting any?"

She swatted his shoulder. "Not in front of the baby."

"Tell me I'm not going as a bee, too," he pleaded, turning her around to look her over.

She peered at him over her shoulder. "Lex went to

the costume shop in Lincoln City for all of us. All they had left for men was hats.''

''So we don't bother with clothes from the neck down?''

''You'd like that, wouldn't you? No, you have a pith helmet. So when the three of us went to town yesterday, I found you a pair of pocket pants on sale. Trevyn has a photographer's jacket you can borrow with all the pockets, and you can wear the boots you wore in Paintbrush. Then you can be a great white hunter.''

He grinned at her. ''A great white hunter who bagged a bumblebee?''

She bumped his arm with her ample bee hip. ''You'll like it when the pollinating starts.''

THE FOLLOWING EVENING the men and the boys were moving tables and chairs around in the big house, Ferdie barking moral support, while Dotty washed serving bowls in the kitchen and kept an eye on Sadie in her infant seat on the counter. Gusty and her sisters finished the decorating. They hung a jointed paper skeleton on the front door, set up a CD player in the hallway with atmospheric Halloween sounds and scattered fall leaves all over the table that would hold the food.

They strung pumpkin lights in several doorways, and Alexis had created a large fabric witch on a broom, a pair of green-and-black-striped socks and black high-heeled pumps sticking straight out ahead of her as she appeared to be sliding down the banister.

Everyone laughed uproariously when she was installed.

Trevyn hooked an arm around Lexie's neck and kissed her temple. "You're a genius and she's a riot. What's her name?"

"Well, I've been calling her Athena while I was working on—"

Another broom that Athena was about to stand in a corner for added atmosphere was suddenly wielded with revenge and struck Alexis on the bottom. "How dare you? Those are *my* Ferragamo pumps!"

Ferdie, sensing a game, wagged his tail and barked.

Alexis barely kept a straight face, both hands on her backside. "I said I called her that while I was *working* on her. What about Mehitabel?"

David took the broom from Athena and stood it in the corner, winking at her. "No vehicles in the house, please."

She gave him a scolding look that he kissed away.

"What about Samantha?" Brandon asked.

"Or Tabitha?" Brady contributed. "Like the old reruns we watch after school."

Trevyn took a vote, and the witch was named Samantha.

The room fell quiet suddenly and Alexis, standing at the foot of the stairs, said to David, "This is just where I was standing the first time I saw you." She pointed several steps up from the bottom. "And that's where we sat while we ate." She looked around at her assembled family and shook her head. "Can you believe how much has changed since that fateful night?''

They all considered that in silence, Brandon and Brady closing in on David and Athena, Trevyn and Alexis, hand in hand, Bram and Gusty, arms wrapped around each other.

''I guess we could say you ladies considering us criminals,'' David said, ''was the best thing that could have happened to all of us.''

Trevyn pointed to the doorway to the dining room. ''I walked out of there with a glass of champagne in each hand, one of them intended for Mrs. Beasley's niece, when I was waylaid by a gorgeous flapper who took possession of one of them—'' he leaned down to kiss the tip of her nose ''—and my heart. Yes. It's been a good thing.''

Gusty could remember that part. ''And I saw a Musketeer standing there,'' she said, pointing to the corner of the room near the conservatory, and was absolutely terrified that I wasn't going to be able to interrogate him as I was supposed to.''

''Funny,'' David said, ''because Bram's the interrogation master. Whenever we had to get a captive to talk, he was the one we used. In camouflage paint, and with those laser eyes, he could always make them spill their guts without ever raising a finger.''

Gusty laughed lightly. ''Well, in my case, he didn't frighten me, but before I knew it I was telling *him* everything about myself and all I'd learned about him was my own conviction that he'd have never done anything to hurt Sadie.''

"Do you remember everything about that night?" Athena asked.

Gusty nodded. "Pretty much. I remember that Lex and I were convinced they couldn't have done anything wrong. You were the only holdout." She grinned at David. "Apparently you don't have quite the charming innocence about you that Bram and Trevyn have."

David laughed. "So it would seem."

"Then Athena and Alexis went home and completely forgot about us until…" David hesitated, apparently mentally reviewing what he knew. "Until Gusty surfaced in the river. But you and Bram reconnected the weekend after the party."

Athena spread her arms. "Who could want more than we all have right now? Have you decided if you're going to stay here, or if you're going back to Pansy Junction?"

"You could teach in Dancer's Beach," Lexie said.

And suddenly those words rang in Gusty's memory as though she'd heard them before.

In a man's voice.

And at high volume!

She concentrated her attention on the image forming in her mind. She and Bram faced each other, clearly in the middle of a heated argument. He was furious and she was crying.

"How could you *ever* have thought that I could father a baby," he demanded, "then not want to raise it because it wasn't perfect?"

"You said you didn't want to have a baby!"

"Well, I didn't think I did, but I certainly had the right to know I had one!"

"I'm telling you now!"

"At seven months along? Isn't that a little late?"

"I just wanted you to know, now that the ultrasound came back negative. But if you're going to keep yelling at me, I'll just be on my—"

"You are not walking away with my baby!" he shouted at her. "We're getting married as soon as we can arrange it."

It took her a moment to realize that nothing was going as she'd expected it to. "No, we're not," she said. "I want to make sure the baby is—"

He talked over her as though she hadn't spoken. "If you want to go back to work after the baby, that's great. You can teach in Dancer's Beach!"

"None of the tests is one hundred percent accurate! What if the baby *is* born with a problem? We should wait!"

And suddenly the major inconsistency in the picture became clear to her. She narrowed her focus on it to make sure she wasn't mistaking its importance.

There was small pink flowered Victorian wallpaper all around them, several pieces of antique or reproduction furniture, French doors that went out onto a little balcony.

They were at the Shelldrake.

Yes. She remembered the Shelldrake. She remembered meeting Bram there.

In the image in her mind he wore brown cords and a brown three-button sweater. Even in her fear and agitation, she was thinking that he looked strong and wonderful. But she'd never seen him this angry before.

It was her own appearance that caused her throat to tighten now, as she realized absently that her sisters and everyone else in the room, including the boys, were watching her worriedly. Even Ferdie whined softly.

She wore the gray plaid jumper that had been one of her favorite pregnancy outfits. And her pregnancy protruded considerably. She was seven months along.

Her throat tightened further and her heartbeat began to thump as she realized that they'd had this argument just before she'd run off on him and ended up in the river.

She felt as though she heard thunder as blood rushed to her brain with the realization of just how complete Bram's deception had been.

"We're getting married as soon as we can arrange it," he'd said.

They hadn't been married then.

So they weren't married now!

As she turned to him, she remembered his easy, smiling claim to all the nonsexual intimacies they'd shared. His convincing stories of all they'd done as a couple. His possessive claim to the baby.

And it had all been lies.

SHE KNEW THE TRUTH.

Bram looked back at her intrepidly as she found

his face in the group gathered around her, watching her in concern.

He'd known this moment would come. He'd tried to prepare for it; he'd even tried to anticipate it—but not hard enough. Now they were going to have to have it out.

He didn't regret it. His actions had led to this moment, but without them, he wouldn't have had the past seven weeks.

And he wouldn't trade them for anything.

She came to stand toe to toe with him and accused without preamble, "We're not married!"

"No," he replied.

She slapped him with a vigor and determination his old hand-to-hand combat instructor would have appreciated. But when she prepared to do it again, he caught her wrist and shackled it.

She swung out with the other and he caught it, too.

"What do you mean, you're not married?" Athena demanded as Gusty struggled against him.

Knowing he'd sustain serious injury if he let go, he turned Gusty around in his arms like a swing dancer, crossing her arms over each other while he continued to hold her hands.

"She broke up with me because she thought I wouldn't want the baby," he explained briefly. "But she and I have to talk about it before we explain it to anybody else. Would you excuse us and keep an eye on the baby for a little while?"

"I'm not sure we should let her go with him!"

Alexis said, getting between him and door. "If he's been lying to her all this time about being married…"

"He had his reasons," Trevyn said, pulling her out of the way. "Let them go."

"What reasons?" she asked. Then she turned on David. "You *knew?*"

"We both knew," Trevyn said. "But they have to talk about it before we can."

"He won't hurt her," David promised Athena, crossing the room to open the door for them.

"It appears he's already *done* that."

"Only because you don't know the whole story."

Bram had to lift Gusty against his side to make any progress toward the door.

"Don't make a liar out of me," David grumbled under his breath.

Bram just kept moving.

Gusty was murderous. Once they were out the door, she screamed at him and kicked, half the blows missing him, the other half making sure he'd never have a career in track and field.

He held on resolutely and kept moving, feeling sorry for his friends, who'd kept his confidence and were now in trouble.

"I hate you!" Gusty screamed at him. "The minute you let me go, Sadie and I will be out of here so fast…!"

"Yeah, yeah, yeah," he said, having to toss her over his shoulder to climb the stairs to the apartment. "But first we're going to make sure you remember everything about what happened!"

He carried her inside, closed and locked the door behind him and flipped on the living room light.

For an instant, he saw it in all it had come to mean to him as a haven of domestic bliss. In a life that had been filled with emotional and physical hardships, these few rooms with his wife and his daughter inside and his best friends only yards away, had been like some undeserved but gratefully accepted reward.

Then he saw her standing in the middle of it, looking as though she'd cheerfully murder him, and knew he had to pull it all out, no matter how much it hurt both of them.

He pointed her to the couch. "Sit down," he said. "I'll make some coffee."

He was most of the way into the kitchen before he realized she had no intention of cooperating.

He caught her on the second stair, grabbed a fistful of the back of her sweatshirt and hauled her back inside. He closed and locked the door again and sat her in the leather chair.

"Okay, forget the coffee," he said, kicking the ottoman with his foot until it was in front of her. He sat on it and looked into her eyes. "What made you remember that we aren't married?"

She drew her feet up and crossed her legs under her, as though she couldn't bear to be that close to him. "I remembered fighting with you at the Shelldrake. I was very advanced in my pregnancy and you were telling me I wasn't walking away with your baby, that we were getting married. *Getting* married!"

She folded her arms and looked away from him. "You liar," she said bitterly.

"Lying was the only option you left me," he said quietly. "I want to make sure you remember that."

"Lying is *never* an option!"

He got a perverse pleasure in throwing that back in her face.

"Now think about that a minute, Gus. What did you do to me when you called me and told me it was over between us?"

"I tried to protect you!"

"Really? By torturing me with the out-of-the-blue news that you didn't love me anymore when we were supposed to be married in two weeks? By telling me that it developed too quickly and just fizzled?"

Her fists were clenched, her arms folded defensively in front of her. She looked like a wild-haired child in a tantrum.

"I didn't say that!"

"I was paraphrasing. I believe you said it wasn't real, that you'd made a terrible mistake and you didn't want me to come to Pansy Junction. You didn't want to see me again."

She drew a breath that sounded like a sob. But she remained dry-eyed and furious. "I'd just gotten the results of the amniocentesis. I thought the baby was going to be impaired."

"And you didn't think I was strong enough to take it."

She focused on him, her eyes filled with accusation. "You told me you didn't want children, remember?

When we talked at the party that night, you said you liked other people's but you didn't think you'd want your own. That you were too tough to be trusted with them.''

He had to give her that, and knew he had no defense against it.

''I was stupid. All I thought about then was what it would demand of me, never realizing all it would give me.''

''And how was I expected to know that?''

''Because you claimed to love me,'' he replied. ''We talked for hours, you lay in my arms four nights in a row while we poured out our souls, and it never occurred to you to give me the chance to be bigger than I thought I could be?''

''I was thinking about the baby!''

''And your only thoughts of me were that I wouldn't be able to measure up to what she might need.''

She sighed and her expression became only slightly less combative. ''You'd told me about your unhappy childhood. I just didn't think I should inflict on you what had every indication of being a difficult life.''

''And, in your infinite wisdom, you made a life decision *for* me?''

She put both hands to her eyes, obviously trying to remember what she'd felt then. She finally dropped her hands to her lap and said with the faintest hint of apology, ''It seemed like the right thing at the time.'' She sighed. ''Maybe I was wrong.''

"No kidding," he said mercilessly. "Do you remember that you were wrong twice?"

A pleat appeared between her eyebrows. "Twice?"

"When you got the good news from the ultrasound at the beginning of your seventh month, you called me, remember?"

She closed her eyes, thinking. "I called you from the pay phone at school. I asked you to meet me somewhere."

He remembered that moment. He'd been elated, thinking she'd come to her senses and decided she loved him after all.

When he'd seen her arrive very pregnant, his temper had ignited.

He realized now that probably hadn't helped the situation, but the fault had been hers.

"You also told me you wanted to meet someplace out of the way. We weren't getting together for my birthday at all, but at your request. So I made reservations on the Long Beach Peninsula."

"And you started yelling at me," she said flatly, "the moment you saw me."

"You were seven months' pregnant and hadn't told me!"

"When I tried to explain, you were still shouting."

"Because you made it clear you had no faith in me as a human being."

"I was trying to protect you!" she said again, tears filling her eyes.

"That wasn't how I read it," he insisted. "Then when you told me the ultrasound was negative for all those problems the amnio test suggested, I wanted to get married. Do you remember your answer?''

A tear fell and she swiped it away. ''Yes. I said I wanted to wait until she was born and we *knew* she was all right.''

''So you still didn't trust me to be able to be a parent to a challenged child.''

She opened her mouth to speak.

''If you're going to tell me one more time that you were trying to protect me, I advise you to think twice about it.''

He thought for a moment that she might burst into tears, but she sat up a little straighter instead and asked coolly, ''And somehow my having done that justifies your kidnapping a sick woman—the victim of a murder attempt that wouldn't have happened if she hadn't known *you*—lying to her about being her husband and holding her hostage for weeks while you filled her beleaguered brain with one lie after another?''

He guessed that summed it up, if a little brutally. ''It seemed like the right thing to do at the time,'' he said, flinging her words back at her.

GUSTY SAT BLOCKED in the chair, his presence on the ottoman, elbows leaning on his knees, preventing her from making an escape. And she wanted to desperately.

What she'd done to him had been stupid and selfish, a direct betrayal of everything love was supposed to promise.

But, then, he'd done the same thing to her. Only his trickery had been even more cruel.

"You filled my mind with lies," she said, "when I had no memory and therefore no way to protect myself against it."

He looked regretful, then shook his head. "Technically, I didn't, Gusty. When you called and said it was over between us and didn't want to see me, I spent the next few months imagining that we'd gotten married as we'd planned, and that we were doing all the things we'd talked about. So what I filled you with were my dreams."

She almost fell for that. It was touching, heartbreaking. But just when she'd thought she'd been reclaiming the past, she wasn't sure what was real and what wasn't.

"You lied to me," she accused again.

"Some of it was true," he disputed.

"You told me *I* proposed to you," she said, "and that isn't true. I remember clearly that *you* proposed, and I turned you down because I was afraid we'd be incompatible."

He nodded. "Yes, the schoolteacher and the spy. It seemed like it shouldn't make sense. But love isn't a logical thing. Remember the night before I left? We had just made love and you were crying because I had to leave. Remember what you said to me?"

She tried hard to put the scene together. There was a certain continuity to her memories now, but it was a little like looking at a strip of negatives. Making it out required careful study.

She saw them in bed, she felt her anguish, saw her bare shoulders and back wrapped in his arms.

"I don't think I could live without you now," she said aloud, hearing her voice in her head and repeating the words. "I was happy alone, but now you've made me need you."

"That's right." Bram tapped her knee when she seemed to lose focus. "And what did you say after that? It was very elementary. Very direct."

She groaned. "I asked you to marry me."

"Yes, you did," he said with obvious satisfaction. "I didn't lie about that."

She angled her chin. "But you did lie when you told me we were married three days later after we had our blood tests."

"I dreamed," he corrected.

She knew how to hurt him. "What about my announcing the baby to you by putting booties in your shoes?"

Pain filled his eyes. That gave *her* satisfaction, which turned instantly to regret when he explained. "I got that story from a buddy I served with. His wife told him about their baby that way. I liked it. So, I dreamed it."

She remembered that she had baked him chocolate chip cookies with pecans during those four days. He had liked to sit with her by the fire and watch her brush her hair. She had told him she'd love to honeymoon on a cruise.

Her anger got a new push when she realized that he'd taken many of the things that had happened and somehow woven them into what he wanted her to believe.

"And you did say you liked my butt in jogging shorts," he said. "That was no lie."

She glared at him. "Well, things are changing. I told you I was feeling differently from the woman I thought I used to be. Now that I remember her, I'm sure."

He nodded. "Yeah. I remember once telling you that you were gentle, kind, trusting and optimistic. That doesn't describe you at this moment, does it?"

"You made me believe for seven weeks that we were married!" she shouted, thoroughly exasperated that she couldn't make him understand how that hurt her.

"Think back," he said reasonably, "to the early morning when I woke you up in the hospital and told you I was taking you away somewhere safe. Do you remember that?"

"Yes, I do," she replied impatiently. "That was *after* I lost my memory."

"Right. Do you remember what I did?"

She rolled her eyes. "You showed me the ring on your hand and told me you were my husband and began the big lie!"

"Would you have come with me if I'd been just some guy in your room in the dark?"

She didn't answer, identifying the question for the trap it was.

"I didn't think so," he said, apparently not needing an answer. "You'd have screamed, I'd have been arrested, and you'd have remained in the hospital. And at the right moment Mendez would have gotten you.''

''Oh, right. You did it to protect me?''

''Does that argument only work for you?''

She groaned in exasperation. ''I think you did it because of that alpha male, possessive streak in you. I was carrying your baby, and this was your opportunity to make me stay with you so you could have her.''

''You're almost right,'' he amended. ''It was so I could have both of you. It was cold-bloodedly deliberate, and while I apologize for having hurt you, I'm without remorse for the rest of it.''

''You decided you wanted us,'' she said, trying to make him see what he seemed unable to grasp, ''and you manipulated the situation so that you could have us. Well, people aren't possessions!''

''The hell they aren't!'' he disputed. ''Not physically, of course, but emotionally you had a grip on me that's still stuck in my gut even while I'd love to throttle you. And once you had our baby, that all just grew. We don't *own* each other, but loving each other makes us belong together.'' He drew a breath and made a deliberate effort to lower his voice. ''And talk about manipulating a situation to have it your way! You told me you didn't love me to get me out of the way.''

''To protect you!''

''Bull! You just didn't want to share her!''

''I didn't know how I was going to deal with it, and I *love* children!'' she sobbed. ''How could I expect you to handle it? There! You happy?'' She got to her feet, unable to believe she'd made that admission. ''Gusty, the earth mother, was terrified!''

He stood with her and caught her arm when she would have run past him. He could see how much that admission cost her. ''But you didn't terminate her. You held on. Even when you weren't one hundred percent sure.''

''It was never that I didn't want her,'' she said, tears coming as that frightening time returned with its fears and anguish. ''It was that I was afraid I wouldn't be good enough, or patient enough.''

''You can't feel guilty about being scared,'' he said softly. ''I can't believe anyone else would have felt any differently.''

''See?'' she said. ''That's what I wanted to save you from.''

''But my job as the man who loves you—'' he gave her arm a little shake ''—was to be there with you— for you. And as Sadie's father, I should have been there for her from the beginning.''

She drew away from him and took a step backward. ''I don't know what to do now,'' she said. ''What we've done to each other just seems to prove that we don't know as much about us as we thought we did. And if we could hurt each other the way we have, maybe we just don't belong together.''

HE DIDN'T KNOW how she could say that, but he knew disputing it wouldn't change anything. She wasn't entirely rational on the subject.

"Fine," he said. Pretending to agree with her might allow her to relax, and she would have to before this could ever be resolved. "I'll go get Sadie."

"Okay." She turned around and walked into the bedroom.

When Bram reached the house, he found her sisters frantic. David and Trevyn looked grim. Ferdie and the boys had gone to bed.

Bram told them the problems in a nutshell, explained briefly how Gusty had kept him in the dark about the baby, and broken up with him when she'd thought Sadie would be born with a birth defect.

Then he explained why he'd told her they were married.

He'd expected instant condemnation, but he suspected his friends had laid some groundwork for him while talking themselves out of trouble for having kept his secret. Athena and Alexis looked at him, then at each other.

"Well, lying's never good," Alexis said. She held the baby and passed her to him. Sadie looked wideawake. "But your motives in doing it were at least as good as hers."

Athena agreed with a nod. "Love makes you do things you'd never consider otherwise."

Dotty was philosophical as she handed him a covered casserole. "It's good that you've brought it all out," she said with a bracing smile. "You'll both feel a little lighter in the morning, and before you know it, you'll be able to talk about it calmly and find solutions."

David and Trevyn walked him out into the cold night, David taking the casserole and carrying it for him. Tomorrow was Halloween, and the wind off the ocean was beginning to feel like winter.

"Anything we can do?" David asked as they made their way slowly toward the garages.

"I don't think so," Bram replied. "We have to work it out. She's just not in the mood to find a solution right now."

"Dotty's right," Trevyn said, tucking Sadie's blanket in tightly as leaves skittered across their path and salt spray struck their faces. "Things will seem better in the morning. Lex and I had a rocky path to get to where we are. But we did it. Just hang in there."

"I think it's a trait they all share because of their mother." David stopped at the bottom of the stairs. "They're almost afraid of who they are, because they know part of them is her. Or at least, it should be. But I don' t see a trace of mean, selfish woman in any of them."

Bram wrapped an arm around David, then Trevyn.

"Thanks, guys," he said, thinking that they were as valuable allies in domestic situations as they were in combat. "I appreciate the empathy."

"We'll expect you both at the party tomorrow," David said, placing the casserole on the flat of Bram's hand. "All the McKeons are coming."

"Yeah," Trevyn added. "And Dori asked me specifically if Gusty would be there. So she can't duck out."

"I'll tell her. Thanks for watching Sadie."

"Anytime." David waved, and he and Trevyn turned back to the big house.

Bram looked down at Sadie in the floodlight on the garage and caught a large, bright smile.

It warmed him to the marrow of his bones.

He had a feeling, though, that if he thought he needed a good night's sleep to deal with Gusty in the morning, he wasn't going to get it.

Sadie had other plans.

Chapter Twelve

Gusty awoke in the middle of the night and listened for the tick of the clock in the cabin's living room. She sat up in surprise when she didn't hear it.

Her bare feet touched carpet rather than bare floor and she drew her foot back as though she'd been stung. Where was she?

Then she remembered. Everything. There was no more cabin, no more hiding out, no more pregnancy.

No more Bram.

She remembered their long, ugly quarrel that got nowhere and solved nothing. She remembered the accusations and counteraccusations.

She remembered she'd finally suggested that what they'd done to each other was proof they didn't belong together.

And he'd said, "Fine." The man who'd tracked her down, made love to her until she was senseless, made her believe he'd married her to make her trust him, kept her and her baby safe—had said "Fine."

She stretched out her hand and felt the vast emptiness of the mattress on his side of the bed. It made her feel cold.

She wanted to hide out somewhere with Sadie until the world stopped confusing her. Maybe at the cabin. She'd loved it there. Bram had loved her there.

But now that she had her memory back, there was just too much confusion. Too much truth to face.

She glanced at the clock. It was almost four in the morning. And Sadie hadn't stirred once?

She got up and crossed the few steps to the crib, certain something must be wrong. She reached down to touch the baby and felt cool, empty blankets. Her heart fell to her feet as her brain made a swift connection.

Bram wanted to be Sadie's father. His side of the bed was cold and the crib was empty! No wonder he'd agreed so willingly that it was over between her and him. What he really wanted was the baby. And he'd taken her!

She ran out of the room shouting, "Bram! Sadie!" heading for the front door in her bare feet, wondering in a panic how much of a head start he had on her.

She hardly noticed that the living room light was on or that soft sounds came from the television until she heard her name.

"Gus?"

She whirled around to see Bram standing on the other side of the kitchen counter, looking surprised by her burst through the room. He wore the same clothes he'd worn when she went to bed and in his arm was a very bright looking Sadie.

Gusty ran around the counter to them and took the baby. Sadie gave her a big, gummy smile.

"I didn't hear her cry," Gusty said. "Did she just get up?"

He shook his head and she noticed for the first time how weary he looked. He was putting the nipple top on a bottle of breast milk she'd expressed.

"No, she hasn't been to bed yet. That's the last time she visits your sisters. I think they give her uppers or something so they can keep playing with her." He held up the bottle. "Are we going to need this, or do you want to feed her?"

She carried Sadie to the sofa, bouncing her, and settled in a corner with her. She unbuttoned the tailored top of her pajamas and started to nurse.

Bram leaned his elbows on the kitchen counter and watched them. "You thought I'd run off with her," he said.

She expected anger, but instead he seemed grimly accepting. "Wouldn't that be out of character for a man you thought *wouldn't* want her?"

She cast him a pleading look. "Bram, it's four o'clock in the morning."

"Actually, Sadie and I discussed it," he said, coming around the counter. "Somewhere around two o'clock, but we decided you'd never make it without us."

"Did you."

"Yes. You need her because you love her. And you need me as a repository for all the things you fear in yourself."

She blinked at him. "Pardon me?"

"You think you shouldn't be afraid of anything," he explained almost amiably. "I suppose because your mother made you believe you were a coward. So you blame me for the things you're afraid of and that means you can pretend to be brave."

She felt her mouth fall open, feelings crushed.

"You were afraid to have a baby that could be very ill or possibly even die—a normal reaction on anyone's part. But you convinced yourself that *I* wouldn't be able to deal with it, because somehow that allows you to feel superior and do the things you're most afraid of."

She stared at him, pain grinding its way through her with large gearlike teeth.

"Then Sadie turns out to be fine, we discover that we're very compatible and can be happy together, but you realize how badly you misjudged me, and punish me instead of yourself by telling me it's over—again."

She continued to stare. That couldn't be true.

"If you're willing to be early-morning shift," he said, indicating the baby eating hungrily, "then I'll go on to bed. I'm meeting a client in the morning."

"Yes," she said stiffly. "Go to bed."

When the door closed behind him, she put her free hand to her eyes where a headache throbbed. God. Had she really done that?

GUSTY WENT TO VISIT Athena and Alexis shortly after eight o'clock. Bram had left for his office at seven.

Dotty answered the door and took the sleeping baby from her. "They're right here, trying to blow up a ghost," she said, pointing toward the middle of the floor where Athena worked, Ferdie hiding behind her as the large, flat plastic ghost twitched. "You join them and I'll bring tea and scones along in a little bit."

That was the best offer she'd had in days. Now all she had to do was make Athena and Alexis understand why she hadn't told them about the baby. At least she had an easy out for not telling them about the wedding. There hadn't been one.

"Hey!" Athena called as she worked a bicycle pump vigorously up and down. "Come lend a hand here. My arms are getting tired and Lexie's such a petunia."

Gusty pulled off her coat and went to join them.

"I am *not* a petunia," Alexis denied with a wink at Gusty. "But now that I've been commissioned to do the Buckley statue for the front lawn of the library, I think I should treat my arms and hands with care."

"Why don't you have them insured," Athena suggested, falling onto her backside on the carpet as Gusty took over. Ferdie continued to watch the action from behind her. "Then we can break them for you for the money."

"Very loving thought, thank you."

"It came from the bottom of Samantha's heart."

Gusty frowned at them over the limp body of the half-inflated ghost as she worked the bicycle pump.

"Stop fighting. I came to give you a few answers," she said.

"To what questions?" Athena asked.

Alexis poked her. "You know. Why she didn't tell us about the wedding and the baby."

"Well, we got the answer to part of that last night." Athena sat cross-legged, her hands on her ankles. "They weren't married. Did you work that out?"

"Sort of," Gusty said, pumping. *I said, "Maybe we shouldn't be together," and he said, "Fine."* Somehow, she didn't want to share that. "I remember why I didn't tell you I was in love."

Alexis stretched her legs out and leaned her weight on her hands, braced behind her. "Why was that?"

"I think, at first, I loved that it had happened," she said, slowing her pumping pace as her arms grew weary. She was encouraged, though, when the ghost's head popped up, filled with air. Ferdie barked a threat, but retreated quickly to the kitchen. "I mean, all he had was my job and he *found* me. And he flew over five hundred miles to tell me that he couldn't get me out of his mind."

"Gusty, stop." Alexis pulled her away from the pump and took over the job. "But if I get too sore to sculpt," she warned Athena, "I'm suing for damages."

Athena grinned. "I know a good lawyer. Go on, Gusty."

Gusty sat between them, rubbing her arms. "We had just those four days together and decided to get married in the spring. He was working on a couple of cases, and I had to put in for the time and prepare for a substitute. And I think I was just so thrilled at first that I liked it being my secret. We decided not to tell anyone so there wouldn't be any fuss. We'd elope, and then we'd share the news.''

"But you didn't get married," Alexis said.

Gusty shook her head, tears springing to her eyes at the memory of that frightening lab report. Slowly she told her sisters what it had said, and what she'd decided to do regarding Bram.

"Sadie's fine, isn't she?" Athena asked.

"Yes. She's perfect. It was all the result of a bad test."

"Gusty, I can't believe you did that to Bram," Athena said. "That's awful."

Gusty looked at her in some surprise. She'd hoped for sisterly empathy and compassion.

"Well, I thought I was protecting him."

"You were making his decision for him."

"That's what he said. But when we'd met at the party, he'd told me he didn't want children. If he didn't want a healthy child, I couldn't imagine how he'd feel about one that might have major problems or even…die."

"But that was his decision to make."

"Well, what about when he told me we were married so that he could have things his way after all?"

Lexie leaned on the pump. "How did that happen, anyway? Bram told us some of this last night, but there were questions I forgot to ask. You're losing me here.''

Gusty explained about calling him after the good news of the ultrasound and asking him to meet her. ''He made reservations at the Shelldrake. He wanted to get married, I wanted to wait and make sure that everything was all right with Sadie. We fought all weekend. We were leaving there when Mendez pushed my car into the river.''

''You wanted to wait,'' Lexie speculated, pumping again, ''because you still didn't trust him.''

''Because,'' she corrected patiently, ''he had a difficult childhood and I wanted him to have an out if he needed one.''

''Letting him believe,'' Lexie argued, ''that you didn't consider him up to what life might require of him.''

She sighed defeatedly. ''Well, pardon me. Maybe there's more of Mom in me than I want there to be. He thinks I transferred my fear of the situation onto him, so that I could feel brave. That makes me at least as good a manipulator as she was.''

''Oh, stop it!'' Athena scolded with a sharp look. ''You're nothing like her. You were faced with a scary situation and you didn't run, but you shored yourself up by knocking the pins out from under *him*. Yet he came to your rescue, kept you and Sadie safe, and from all indications, has treated you like a loving husband. You can't possibly be thinking of walking away from all that?''

"I think he's the one who'd probably be relieved to go," Gusty said.

Athena shook her head at her. "You're doing it again. You're the one who wants out because he's proven himself to be bigger than you are."

"Yeah," Alexis said, kneeling up to lean hard on the pump. "Just suck it up, tell him you're sorry and grateful for all he's done, and promise things will be different from now on."

"You both seem to be forgetting," she insisted irritably, "that he also lied to me."

"So that he could look out for you," Athena countered. "You lied to him to make things easier on you."

Gusty gasped, horrified that she could be so misunderstood.

Athena surprised and confused her by putting an arm around her. "I know. It was easier to bear it all yourself than to watch him suffer, too. You meant well, but it was wrong."

Gusty put both hands to her face and burst into tears.

Athena held her close.

Dotty walked in with a tea tray and demanded anxiously, "What have you two done to the poor girl now?"

At last, Gusty thought. Someone was on her side!

BRAM GLANCED at the antique Regulator clock on his office wall. Almost nine-thirty. His client was due at any moment.

There'd been a message left in a woman's raspy voice on his answering machine yesterday morning, asking for help in a missing persons case. Missing persons, he thought wryly, considering Gusty's situation, was getting to be big business in Dancer's Beach.

He'd come to his downtown office two and a half hours early, hoping to distract his despair with paperwork, but instead he'd taken up the time with worry. What if he couldn't turn Gusty around? What if she did try to leave with the baby? What would he do? How could he go on?

He could threaten her with claiming custody because his name was on the birth certificate. But he wasn't sure he could make her any more unhappy than she was already.

He'd thought he'd have to live without her before, he reminded himself, and he'd survived. He could do it again. But he had to stop himself from remembering how miserable those five months had been.

He went to the window to look out on the park across the street. It was cold and overcast today, but children bundled up against the weather played on the slide and swings, their mothers watching from the benches.

People wandered in and out of the library, and traffic moved slowly on Dancer Avenue as shoppers hurried by, probably for last-minute purchases of candy and other goodies for trick-or-treaters.

"Mr. Bishop?" a woman's soft voice said from behind him.

He turned—and stopped, unable for a moment to speak. A slender woman dressed entirely in black stood in the open doorway, a cigarette in one hand, sunglasses covering her eyes, and over them a sort of veil that seemed to be part of a little black derby hat partially concealed her nose.

He felt like Marlow or Sam Spade being visited by some eccentric character seeking his services.

He cleared his throat and remembered his manners—and his business. "Mrs. Delacroix?" he asked.

"Oui," she replied, putting the cigarette to her lips.

Hoping this meeting would be conducted in English, he went to stand behind his client's chair. "Please come in."

She drew on the cigarette, walked elegantly toward the chair and sat with easy grace. Then she coughed loudly and patted her chest. She looked for somewhere to put out her cigarette.

He dumped his paper clips out onto the blotter and handed her the shallow pottery bowl that had held them.

"Merci," she said, and stubbed out the weed. *"Mon Dieu,"* she said with a smile, "but you are *très beau,* Monsieur L'Eveque."

Très beau, he repeated to himself worriedly. Very something.

"I'm also *très* American," he said, taking his chair and smiling apologetically across his desk. "Do you speak English?"

"Yes, I speak English," she said, with no trace of an accent and a sudden seriousness she seemed to regret. She reached behind her to pull a pin from her hat and remove it. She placed it on her crossed knee. "It's Halloween, isn't it? I was playing a role, and I was rather getting into it. Much as you've done, I understand."

It had been a long, sleepless night, but he was beginning to feel as though they weren't having the same conversation—in English or in French.

And there was something curious about her voice.

"You called about locating someone for you," he said, trying to bypass what he didn't understand.

"Yes. My family."

"They're missing?"

"No, they're right here in Dancer's Beach. I just need you to help me get to them."

The soft, sophisticated sound of her voice was needling his memory, but he couldn't imagine why.

"I don't understand," he said frankly. "If you know they're here, why can't you simply go to them?"

"Because I'm dead, honey." She took off her glasses and smiled at him, and he knew instantly who she was.

She couldn't be, but she was.

"Auntie?" he asked in disbelief.

She smiled and reached across the desk to pat his hand. "Your very own Halloween ghost, sweetie."

Laughing, he pushed himself away from his desk and stood. She got to her feet and walked into his arms. "Oh, Bram. So this is what you look like. I'm sorry about the subterfuge, but since I was buried, you can understand why I can't just walk through town, greeting everyone.''

''Are you in protective relocation?'' he asked, seeing her back into her chair. ''What happened?''

She reached long slender fingers into the sides of a short graying red bob and stretched her arms. ''Oh, it feels as though it's been forever! I did another job after the three of you quit. Turned out to involve Pavel Yevgeny, that double agent from the arms deal when the wall came down, remember?''

He nodded.

''He recognized me from a surveillance photo,'' she said with a philosophical shrug. ''We got him and put him away, but not before he blew my cover. They got me out and set me up as a milliner in Paris. Angeline Delacroix.''

''I can't believe it,'' he said, still trying to absorb the fact that she was sitting across the desk from him. ''David's loving the house. He married Athena.''

She nodded, smiling. ''I know. I've kept tabs on all of you. I left David the house, knowing the girls would never sit still for it. They're a smart and beautiful bunch, but their egos were so damaged by their mother that all they'd do is work. I was afraid they'd never find men, fall in love, get married. So I did what I could to bring that about.'' She heaved a sigh of satisfaction.

''But how did you know what was going on?'' he asked in surprise.

''You don't think Wren works for the three of you exclusively, do you? I know David's brothers live with him, Trevyn married Alexis, and you…'' She studied him with a judicious expression. ''You're in love with Gusty.''

He groaned quietly. ''It's very complicated.''

She nodded knowingly. ''I talk to Wren, Wren talks to David…'' Her eyes welled with tears and, after a hard swallow, she said, ''The two of you have a daughter named Sadie.''

''You're very well informed.'' He offered her a tissue. ''But you have to see her to know how beautiful she is.''

''I can't wait. I know everything you've told David about the scary results of that test, about your pretending to be married, about your quarrels since. What I don't know is what you intend to do about Gusty.''

He didn't know himself. ''My best'' was all he could tell her.

She slapped the desktop. ''And if that's always been good enough for the U.S. government, I guess it's good enough for me.'' She leaned an elbow on the desk. ''Now, how are you going to get me to the house tonight without letting everyone see me? Even in costume, I can't take the chance of running into friends and neighbors.''

''I'll run you up the back stairs after dark,'' he said, ''and into that sitting room off David's bedroom. Used to be your bedroom.''

She smiled wistfully. ''Ah, yes. I used to read to the girls there. I'm so anxious to see them. It's against all the rules, but I have to see the happiness in their faces for myself or I'll never rest.''

"Leave it to me.''

GUSTY SAW BRAM in the shadows with a woman in a flowing, hooded cape. He'd called from the office to say he wouldn't be home for dinner and would meet her at the party.

She hadn't even thought about the possibility of him knowing women in Dancer's Beach. Still, even though he worked away a lot, he'd spent a considerable amount of time here. And for five months he'd considered their relationship over, so it wasn't surprising that he'd have established other relationships.

It was just a little startling that he'd switched allegiance so quickly. And that he'd sneak another woman up the back steps of Cliffside at a party hosted by Gusty's family and his friends.

And a hooded cape was such a shameless bid for drama even if it was a costume party.

Why was she surprised by Bram's behavior? Hadn't his final words to her last night been that she had two alternatives? They could part company, or she could admit that she wasn't always perfect? He'd apparently presumed she'd chosen the first.

She watched as the caped woman flung her arms around him and held him tightly.

She saw tenderness in his embrace. The tenderness he'd once shown her and she'd failed to appreciate until too late.

And here *she* was dressed like a bumblebee.

She yanked off her costume and tossed it in David's bathroom, definitely out of the partying mood. She brushed bee fuzz off her black slacks and smoothed the sleeves of her black sweater. If she spent the evening helping Dotty in the kitchen, no one would notice that she was out of costume.

She felt a sudden and overwhelming need to cry. She fought it bravely for about a minute, then went into the bathroom to succumb.

"Was the deceased someone you knew?"

Gusty looked up guiltily at the sound of Bram's voice. He stood in the bathroom doorway and pointed to the bee parts scattered across the floor.

She couldn't speak. Grief, disappointment, anger all clogged in her throat.

"Obviously a nuclear-entomological experiment gone wrong," he said, insisting on carrying on with the joke.

She applied a cold washcloth to her face and made herself cut her losses. "Obviously," she replied. "Experiments gone wrong all over the place tonight."

He leaned in the bathroom doorway, looking very much like the great white hunter she'd tried to create, though he'd apparently chosen to doff the pith helmet.

"You just now getting in costume?" he asked.

"I just got out," she said, reaching into her purse for her cosmetics bag. "It was too hot."

"Can you still pollinate without it?"

He was determined to torture her. "I'll let you know." She reapplied blush, powder, then touched up her mascara.

Then perversely, the moment she looked almost civilized, her eyes filled again, tears spilled over and smeared her eye makeup.

She yanked a tissue from the box on the shelf and glared at Bram.

BRAM WASN'T ENTIRELY SURE what was going on here. During the past twenty-four hours, she'd been angry at him, exasperated with him, crushed that he'd lied to her.

He and Aunt Sadie had spent all afternoon in his office, talking about Gusty and her sisters, and she'd suggested that Gusty's anger with him could be more that they weren't married than because he'd made her believe they were.

He wondered if that was true, because there seemed to be a sadness attached to her attitude that hadn't been there last night or this morning. Or maybe it was just the black she was wearing that made her appear pale and thin, the skinned-back hair that made her eyes enormous.

No. He'd just seen tears in her eyes. Something new had happened.

"You know, it would help," she said, wiping off the eye stuff again, "if you weren't staring at me while I do this."

"What are you crying about?" he asked intrepidly. "If you're planning to do something that makes you unhappy, you shouldn't do it."

"Well, it appears I'm not going to have a choice," she said, sniffing and applying new stuff.

"About what?"

"About what," she repeated hotly as she scooped her makeup into the bag she held open right under the shelf. She missed and it fell to the floor. The mascara rolled under the tub. "What are we talking *about?*" she demanded. "We're talking about you, that's what! What choice have you left me?"

She got down on her knees and reached an arm under the tub, groping for the tube of black stuff.

He'd thought conducting a conversation half in French was difficult!

Under other circumstances, he'd have enjoyed watching her tightly clad derriere while she searched for her makeup, but he wanted to clear things up between them even more than he wanted the view.

He put two fingers in the waistband of her jeans and tugged.

She came up like a rabid cat. "Don't you *dare* touch me!" she screamed at him, her expression furious but in clear danger of crumpling. "I know I was stupid! I know I was wrong! But if you can turn around and…and…"

She didn't get to finish.

The sitting room door burst open and Athena and Alexis appeared, followed by David and Trevyn.

She didn't have to finish. He finally understood what had happened. She'd seen him from the window with Aunt Sadie and leaped to a faulty conclusion.

"…rude to leave our guests," Athena was saying as Gusty glared at Bram from the shelter of the bathroom. "If you have a surprise for us, I don't see why we can't have it downstairs."

"Because it's a private surprise," David said practically. Bram had pressed his friends into service.

"We did that before the party," she said, and laughed. "Can't you wait until *after* to do it again?"

"No," he replied frankly, "but that's not the surprise."

"Then what is it?" Alexis asked with a sigh. "I was having a very nice discussion with Rhett Butler and I think it was going to lead to some contraband chocolates."

"Just sit down," Trevyn said. "Bram should be here any minute."

Bram enjoyed the confusion in Gusty's eyes.

He caught her arm and pulled her out into the sitting room. "Hi," he said to their companions. "We're here."

"Gusty, what is going on?" Athena asked. "What are they talking about? What surprise?"

She shook her head. "I don't know, but I don't think I'm included so I'll…" She started for the door, but Bram caught her arm and drew her back.

"You're included. Where are Dotty and the boys?"

"Here!" Brady burst in, eyes wide and uncertain.

Brandon and Dotty followed, Ferdie at their heels.

"I didn't mean it," Brady said anxiously as David went behind him to close the door.

"Mean what?" David asked.

"The pumpkin."

"What pumpkin?"

Brady looked around at the collection of family, then up at David. "This is not about the pumpkin?"

David was now suspicious. "No."

Brady smiled innocently. "Then, never mind."

"Actually, this is sort of about a pumpkin," Bram said, pushing Gusty into a chair as David led Dotty to the chair he'd occupied and urged the boys to curl up on the floor with the dog, "if you consider the pumpkin-turning-into-a-coach fairy tale. We've all sort of got Cinderella stories going here, from three guys who've seen it all and had begun to think there was nothing left to fight for, until we met the three of you."

He encountered Athena's and Alexis's smiling faces and Gusty's baffled one.

"To Dotty, Brady and Brandon, who were smart enough to know they wanted to live here."

Everyone stared at him. Waiting.

He didn't know how to prepare them for how good this was going to be.

"This is one of those gifts life seldom presents. Something or someone lost is usually lost forever."

He went to the back door onto the stairs and opened it. The woman in the cape that Gusty had seen through the window walked into the room.

Gusty looked horrified.

He brought the woman into the middle room.

"Unless you're Sadie Richmond," Bram said. "And then you come back to life. Dave, Trev, meet Auntie."

Chapter Thirteen

Gusty heard her sisters scream, saw them leap up in a blur to embrace Aunt Sadie, heard Ferdie bark as everyone reacted with excitement. But she didn't seem to be able to move or speak. The grief that had stayed with her since she'd remembered Sadie's "death" exploded into a million pieces at the sight of her aunt's smiling face.

But her body felt paralyzed, sort of weighted down with joy.

Strong arms pulled her up and steadied her as Athena and Alexis held Sadie between them and laughed and cried.

"You all right?" Bram asked.

"I'm not sure," she whispered. She could feel herself shaking.

Bram turned to David. "How about a shot of brandy, Dave?"

David took one look at her face and hurried to the small liquor cabinet across the room. He poured a jigger and brought it to her.

Bram put it to her lips.

She took a small sip and felt its burning warmth slip down into her stomach.

"Another one," he encouraged.

She'd just swallowed a third sip when her sisters suddenly remembered her and turned to draw her into their embrace with Sadie.

Sadie, looking youthful and beautiful and so reassuringly full of life, put a diagnostic hand to her cheek. "Oh, Gusty. We shouldn't have shocked you like this. Bram told me what you've been through!"

"Sadie, I'm so happy to see you," Gusty said, wrapping her arms around her and holding her until she was convinced she actually stood there—real and alive. "But I don't understand!"

Sadie explained about being recognized on her last mission and relocating to Paris. About keeping in touch with them through Wren and learning that things had gone just as she'd hoped—that her three beloved nieces had married her three favorite men.

"I left the house to David," she said with her audacious smile, "because I knew you three would have to come and check him out. And that wherever he was, Trevyn and Bram wouldn't be far behind. I hadn't imagined they'd all be here together. Now, where are David and Trevyn?"

The men hugged her in turn and there was great seriousness and some laughter as they recalled cases and people they'd had in common.

David introduced his brothers and Dotty.

Sadie put a hand to each boy's cheek. "Well, you

both look very smart. What are you going to be when you're adults?''

"A writer," Brandon said without hesitation.

"A mechanic who invents things," Brady said. "Brandon says there isn't such a thing, but if there isn't, I'll be the first one."

"Excellent!" she praised. "I love men who know their own minds. Now where's the baby?" Sadie looked around her.

Gusty went to David's bedroom where she'd placed the infant seat in the middle of a large chair. She hurried back to Sadie with it.

"This is your namesake," she said, a catch in her voice. "And I think she's going to be as beautiful as you are."

"Oh. Can I take her out of the carrier."

"Of course."

"What if I wake her up?"

"I don't think you will," Gusty said. "She had Bram up all night and Dotty and me going all morning. She should sleep for hours."

As though aware that it was an auspicious moment, baby Sadie opened her eyes, looked into the eyes of the woman staring at her with adoration, then dropped long, feathery eyelashes and went back to sleep.

Aunt Sadie wept. And so did her nieces.

After a long moment, Sadie handed the baby back to Gusty. She reached down to pet the dog, who seemed to appreciate the commotion Sadie had caused.

"The bad news," she said briskly, "is that I have to go."

A unanimous protest began that she quieted with a raised hand. "I shouldn't even have done this, but Wren told me you were all happy, and I wanted to see it for myself. I helped raise these wonderful women, praying that each lost little soul would find her way. Then I worked with the three of you—" she smiled at David, Trevyn and Bram "—and so admired that even in the darkest moments and in the ugliest places, you always knew what to do. You always looked out for one another, and always found a way home. I wanted my girls to make their homes with you."

Unconsciously, they'd paired off, David and Athena with the boys standing close, Trevyn and Alexis always arm in arm. Bram and Gusty with little Sadie, standing side by side but not touching.

"Man-woman love is a miracle," she said gravely to Gusty. "I had it once for such a short time, and then it was gone. I'll never feel that magic again. To deny it is criminal. Even sacrilege."

Then she hugged everyone in turn and took one last look around the room. "If anyone should decide to vacation in Paris, there's a little millinery shop on the Rue Combon. You'll find me there." Her lip quivered and she put her hood up.

"How will you get back?" Athena asked anxiously.

"Wren brought her," Bram said. "He's waiting outside."

She blew a kiss into the room and was gone.

There was silence for a long moment, then Alexis turned to her weeping sisters and sniffed. "The thing to remember is that she's alive!"

Athena nodded. "And she's an excuse to go to Paris."

"Who needs an excuse?" Alexis asked. "I know all the best places. We'll start planning a trip right after the party." She turned to Gusty. "Are you in?"

"Of course," she replied.

"Okay, I hate to be a killjoy," David said, "but we have a houseful of guests who are getting zero attention at the moment."

"Actually, some of them are cleaning up pumpkin," Brady said as he followed David out the door, "and the others are trying to put that little table thing near the fireplace back together. You know, the one you like so much because it's fitted together instead of..."

His voice faded as David followed him and Brandon into the hallway, Dotty trying to hurry past them to assess the damage, Ferdie nudging the backs of knees to get through first.

Athena lingered to hug Alexis, then Augusta. "You coming?" she asked.

Alexis wiped a hand across her face. "Am I my usual gorgeous self or do I look blotchy and swollen."

"Gorgeous," Trevyn told her at the same moment that Athena replied, "Blotchy and swollen."

Alexis swatted her arm, then turned to Gusty and

Bram. "You two can't come," she said gravely, "until you work everything out."

"To our satisfaction," Athena added. She followed Alexis and Trevyn into the hall and closed the door.

Alone in the sitting room with Bram, Gusty became aware of the loud, demanding silence. It called for words of apology, of understanding and forgiveness. But despite Bram's tenderness of a moment ago, he turned his back on her and walked to the window.

"You thought I was already fooling around with someone else," he said mildly, holding the draperies back and looking down on the driveway.

Her knees felt weak and she sank onto the sofa. "Yes, I did. You held her as though you really cared."

"I do." He let the draperies fall into place and wandered back toward her. "Sadie always had the information we needed, and she saved our hides a time or two. And she never kicked me in the shins."

Unsure whether he'd said that as an attempt at humor or simply as an accusation, Gusty thought it wisest not to smile. He looked like a man at the end of his rope. And he *had* to understand and forgive her. He *had* to want her to stay.

"You never saw her in person until today," she said. "Actually, her flash point is even lower than mine."

"Mmm." He sprawled in the opposite corner of the sofa, his legs stretched out, his eyes facing the door. "Considering yours, that would give her a minus reading on the flash point scale."

"You're sometimes impatient," she said reasonably.

"Usually when you're around to provoke me."

She angled her body toward the long space that separated them, almost afraid to ask the question but knowing she had to. "Is that what you want?"

He turned his head in her direction. "What?"

"For me not to be around to provoke you?"

She had no idea that much man could move with that much speed. He'd closed the distance between them in a blur of movement and now had her by the shoulders, the two of them kneeling on the sofa, looking into each other's eyes. He glared, she stared.

"Right!" he shouted at her. "That's why I moved heaven and earth to find you, felt as though I would die when you told me it was over, was ecstatic to learn we were going to have a baby and could have cheerfully throttled you when I learned you'd put me off because you were afraid she wouldn't be perfect."

"It wasn't because—" She tried to interject, but he cut her off with a quick shake that rattled her teeth.

"I'm not finished yet," he said ominously.

She swallowed. "Then, do go on."

"That's why I leaped into the water after you," he continued in the same furious tone, "risked arrest to kidnap you from the hospital, hid out with you for almost a month in the middle of nowhere, stood between you and Mendez and his thugs, then faced your *sisters!* It's also why I made you believe we were married—because *I don't want you around!*" The last was issued right in her face, then he let her go and added more quietly, "Yeah. That makes sense."

That was about a quintuple negative, but she thought she got the point. She couldn't quite believe it, but she understood. He was still crazy about her.

"Why don't you just say you love me?" she asked, still afraid to smile.

"Because you're deaf!" He got to his feet and paced the room. "I've said it over and over in a hundred different ways and you don't hear me!"

She winced at the volume. "I can hear you now."

He gave her a dangerous look for her attempt at levity. "Don't," he warned.

She pushed off the sofa and went to stand toe to toe with him, drunk with her new knowledge. She had two miracles in her life named Sadie. And in spite of all the ways in which she'd hurt Bram, he loved her still.

"Are you finished shouting?" she asked, putting a hand to either side of his waist.

His arms were folded across his chest. He didn't budge and he didn't look at her. "For the time being."

"Then I can speak?" she asked innocently.

He cast her a quick look that told her she couldn't fool him with attempts at subservience. "If you think you can make sense."

She smiled into his disgruntled expression. "My irrational behavior is all your fault," she said. "I do things for people. That's my style. I understand my sisters, so I explain them to each other and help them get along. I spend my time with little children who have to be watched and protected every moment." She sighed and made an admission. "I haven't known that many men. I met you, fell in love, and tried to save you from all the things that could hurt you." She swallowed quickly as memories of that time poured back. "All the things that were hurting me." She tossed her head briskly. "I'm into mothering. I'm sorry."

She poked him in the chest with her index finger. "And you should talk, buster. Every time I make a move I feel as though I have an entire platoon behind me with smart bombs or something, ready to defend me from whatever threatens me."

"Keeping the peace and protecting the innocent is what I've always done," he said, with no sign of repentance. "And I'm your husb—" He stopped when he realized he'd pretended one too many times. "I was *supposed* to be your husband. Like it or not, that's the way nature ordained it. I'm tougher than you are, so I should be the one walking point."

"Okay." She nodded and smiled amiably.

He was clearly suspicious of her compliance. "What do you mean?"

"I mean," she explained dutifully, "that while you're walking point, I'll follow with the baby and the food. Or do you call it grub? Chow?"

"Rations," he said, trying to read her eyes.

She let him see how much she loved him. "But I may occasionally stop to tango."

He was beginning to relent. She saw a flash of amusement in his eyes. "You don't know how."

"That didn't stop me before. Well, are you going to do it?"

"Tango?"

"Propose."

"You're the one who broke us up." He unfolded his arms and cupped her elbows in his hands. She drew her first even breath since they'd been left alone. "I think *you* should propose."

"But I did it the last time. And you're walking point, remember? You get to do the tough stuff."

"Okay." His hands moved up to frame her face. She felt a little frisson of sensation down her neck and through her breasts. "But a good soldier always does reconnaissance before taking on a tough assignment."

She waited. This was going to be good.

He kissed her, mouth open, hands roaming, approach possessive and confident. When she melted in his arms, his hand at her bottom held her up against him, reminding her that in a few short days...

And that was when their lovemaking history came back to her in a rush. She saw the two of them in a tangle, one breath, one heartbeat, mouths avid, bodies unable to get close enough though they were flesh to flesh. She felt the hot passion, the unutterable tenderness, the love that now defined them.

She drew away, tears in her eyes and her throat. She'd almost thrown all that away!

"Will you marry me?" she demanded urgently.

"I thought I was sup—" he began, looking surprised.

"Will you?"

"Yes!"

Bram took the change of terms in stride. He was growing accustomed to not knowing what was going on in her head. But why were there tears in her eyes?

"What, Gus?" he asked, still holding her.

"I just remembered us," she said, her voice a whisper. "Making love." She tightened her grip on his neck and buried her nose in his collar. "I think if I could have remembered that sooner, I'd have understood everything. I'm so sorry."

He pressed her closer. "There's no need to be sorry anymore. We were both wrong, but only because we loved each other. I think that's an automatic second chance."

"I love you," she said with all the sincerity he'd ever hoped to hear in the words.

"I know." He squeezed her and kissed her temple. "I love you, too."

She raised her head to look at him. "You'd better call your sister and tell her she's invited to a wedding. Should we do it at Thanksgiving, so she can stay for the holiday?"

He shook his head. He couldn't possibly wait that long. "This weekend. We'll have Thanksgiving early. I suppose we'd better go tell your sisters."

"They're probably listening at the door right now," she guessed.

"We are not!" came in muffled tones from the hallway.

Epilogue

"How come there are more people in the wedding party," Sheila, Bram's oldest niece, wanted to know, "than there are in the church?" She pointed to Peg, Charlie and Dori McKeon on the bride's side, and Dotty on the groom's.

"Because it's a special wedding," Athena replied. She wore a soft plum color and a coronet of ivory and lavender tea roses atop her elegant twist. She was a maid of honor.

Alexis, also a maid of honor, wore a different style dress in eggplant, ivory and pink roses woven into her long hair. "No one wants to sit and watch. Everyone wants to be part of it."

"Right." Lisa Carmichael, Bram's sister, wore a winter-gold dress she'd brought with her, and the same coronet on her short, dark hair. "This is a family of action."

Gusty loved her already. She was warm and funny and bore none of the scars one would have expected from such a childhood.

"Because Bram protected me from them," she explained to Gusty during a quiet moment. "He could have left and made it on his own, but he stayed to get me through. I hope you appreciate how special he is."

"I do," Gusty assured her. "That's why I proposed to him."

Lisa smiled. "Good men are hard to find these days, yet this family seems to have cornered the market.

Frank, Gusty had learned, was gentle and quiet and watched his girls like a hawk when they went out to play on the lawn. The bushes protected them from the drop to the ocean, but he knew children, he said. They could create danger out of nothing.

Obviously another point man.

The girls, Cheryl, Sharon and Sheila, were six, eight and ten, dark and lively, and a source of wonderment and constant blushes to Brandon and Brady. They were now dressed in matching berry-colored dresses, the same roses in their hair.

Alexis tugged at the sleeve of the simple ivory silk dress she'd lent Gusty. "Don't spill punch on this," she warned. "It's my gallery openings dress."

"I wouldn't think of it."

In Gusty's hair were all silver roses.

The organist intoned the Wedding March.

The attendants gathered into quick formation, the girls in the front followed by their mother, and Athena and Alexis, side by side.

Gusty took Sadie from her stroller and stepped into

place behind her sisters. They'd trimmed Sadie's white blanket with white ribbons and flowers, as though she were a bouquet.

"You ready?" David whispered to her as Lisa's girls started up the aisle.

She took his arm. "I am. Thanks for giving me away."

"Happy to. Particularly since I get you right back again as a sister-in-law."

Gusty watched the women in her family moving up the aisle, Bram, Trevyn, Frank, Brandon and Brady waiting at the front of the church, and marveled at the richness of her life. The woman who'd only weeks ago wondered about her place in life now knew where it was. Right beside Bram, and in the middle of their loud, lively family.

As she started up the aisle, she looked down at the baby and whispered softly, "We're getting married."

Sadie gave her a wide, gummy smile.

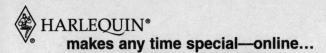

From bestselling
Harlequin American Romance author

CATHY GILLEN THACKER

comes

TEXAS VOWS

A McCABE FAMILY SAGA

Sam McCabe had vowed to always
do right by his five boys—but after
the loss of his wife, he needed the small-town security
of his hometown, Laramie, Texas, to live up to that
commitment. Except, coming home would bring him
back to a woman he'd sworn to stay away from.
It will be one vow that Sam can't keep....

On sale March 2001

Available at your favorite retail outlet.